WALKING

on the

CEILING

WALKING
on the
CEILING

Ayşegül Savaş

RIVERHEAD BOOKS
NEW YORK
2019

RIVERHEAD BOOKS
An imprint of Penguin Random House LLC
penguinrandomhouse.com

Library of Congress Cataloging-in-Publication Data

Names: Savas, Aysegül, author.
Title: Walking on the ceiling / Aysegül Savas.
Description: New York : Riverhead Books, 2019.
Identifiers: LCCN 2018019889 (print) | LCCN 2018023114 (ebook) |
ISBN 9780525537434 (ebook) | ISBN 9780525537410
Classification: LCC PR9165.9.S28 (ebook) |
LCC PR9165.9.S28 W35 2019 (print) | DDC 823/.92—dc23
LC record available at https://lccn.loc.gov/2018019889

Printed in the United States of America
1   3   5   7   9   10   8   6   4   2

Book design by Daniel Lagin

To Maks

Who at such a time
has come to the edge of the doorway?

Apollodorus

WALKING
on the
CEILING

1.

For a short time when I lived in Paris, I was friends with the writer M. He was a foreigner to the city, too, which may have been one reason for our friendship. We went on walks around the city and we wrote to each other.

What remains of that time is a photograph of M. standing in front of a marble wall, looking at me with bewildered eyes. Above his raised eyebrow, a pale and jagged scar rises, deepens, disappears.

Actually, this may not be a scar at all, but a trick of the shadows, or the author's face folded with age. I do not recall a scar from our walks, but I often walked alongside him with my head down. And I'm not sure whether his eyes are really cast up in surprise, as I said, and not simply with impatience at having his photo taken.

Still, I remember M. as always a bit bewildered, and with the scar on his eyebrow—a sign illuminated in that brief moment of documentation when he looked me straight in the eyes.

But here, too, my account is faulty, since between my eyes and his stood the comforting length of the camera lens. As far as I can remember, I never looked M. in the eyes, even when we were seated across from each other at a café.

Some days, it's difficult to believe that this friendship really existed—with its particular logic, its detachment from the world. What I remember has the texture of a dream, an invention, a strange and weightless suspension, like walking on the ceiling.

In my childhood, I would hold a square mirror up to the ceiling. I examined every inch of this flat, white expanse, entirely removed from the jagged world on the opposite pole where people lived in shadows, weighed down by troubles. I understood that all anyone can do in the midst of darkness is retreat to their own, bright landscapes.

I THINK MORE AND MORE THESE DAYS THAT I SHOULD SET DOWN some of the facts of my friendship with M., to keep something of this time intact. But stories are reckless things, blind to everything but their own shape. When you tell a story, you set out to leave so much behind. And I have to admit that there is no shape in those long walks and conversations, even if I think of them often.

Let me place the photograph here, as the tangible remains of our friendship.

What follows is an incomplete inventory.

2.

met M. some months after I moved to Paris from Istanbul. I arrived in the city without a job or a place to live. I was enrolled in a literature program in order to obtain a visa, but I knew even before I came that I would not attend any of the classes.

I had enrolled in the same program once before, a few years after I graduated from university in England. I had a different vision of myself then, and I worked steadily to achieve it. I was living in London with my boyfriend, Luke, and putting together my life piece by piece. I imagined that Luke and I would move to Paris, become its natives, and lead the kind of creative life attributed to the residents of the city. We even spoke to each other in French while we cooked dinner, in preparation for our new life.

On the phone, my mother had urged me to go to Paris. I

hadn't been back to Istanbul for several years and she always found a way to make this sound natural.

"Of course you should go, Nunu," she said. "What's there for you in Istanbul, anyway?"

I hadn't proposed returning home as an alternative.

It wasn't from my mother but from her aunts that I found out she was sick. I went back to Istanbul soon after this, canceling my Paris plans.

The second time I decided to go to Paris, my mother's aunts, Asuman and Saniye, warned me that it was foolish to live a life without roots. It was the type of thing they might have told my mother as well, the type of thing that would have made her silent. The aunts said I should be wise and build myself a life in Istanbul, as if building a life were a matter of simple engineering, as I, too, used to believe. A steady job, an easy commute, a reliable husband.

"Your poor mother never managed," the aunts said.

To build my life, I should have them nearby to make sure everything was done the right way. They wouldn't allow anyone to think that I led the drifting life of an orphan. When the time came, they would arrange for wedding presents, bed linens, tablecloths, dinners.

They even offered to help renovate my mother's apartment.

"We can make it just the way you want," they said, and told me about their plans. We would paint my mother's bedroom and change all the furniture. We would move my bedroom to my mother's study, where she had kept all my father's books. Once we took down the bookshelves, they assured me, the room would actually be very spacious.

My childhood bedroom would serve as a guest room for now.

"And later," Saniye said, "who knows."

They also said, on the afternoon when we went to the notary to finalize the sale of the apartment, that it was a waste. I had already told them I would use some of the money to go to Paris and pay for the program and my living expenses.

They said it again after I signed the papers. "What a waste. Your poor mother's home."

This was a name they gave her afterwards—my poor mother.

3.

In Paris, I moved into a studio apartment close to the Gare du
Nord train station, where frequent arrivals and departures gathered and dispersed people at every moment like a beating heart.
I liked to think that I could board a train and leave the city any-
time I wanted. The neighborhood disassembled itself and came
back together several times a day and was an entirely different
place at night. I did not feel in those first weeks that I was living
in the city, but in the residues of many places.

I was renting the studio from a man who owned the Café du
Coin at the entrance to the building. After our brief meeting at
the café, he carried my single suitcase up the uneven wooden
stairs and unlocked the door.

"If you need anything . . . ," he said at the threshold. Then he
seemed to change his mind and went back downstairs.

My room was bare but not neat, as if someone had moved out

and left behind belongings no longer needed in their new life. There was a mattress, a square table, a stove with a kettle, and four mismatched chairs. I had brought photographs, a small vase, and two porcelain statues from Istanbul and I put them around the room for decoration when I arrived. They seemed tiny and pathetic, and after several days, I put them back into my suitcase.

From my window, I saw a new pile of abandoned furniture on the sidewalk each day, for a municipal truck to pick up. Men in long and colorful tunic shirts would stop by to examine the pieces before walking up the road to congregate around the station to watch the new arrivals to the city.

In the afternoons, I walked down to boulevard de Sébastopol, where I stopped at a grocery store called Istanbul-Grill-Foods to buy a pack of roasted chickpeas. I followed the boulevard south, to the Seine, with the thought that I would walk to the neighborhoods of the Left Bank, or along the river to the gilded monuments—all the places that appeared in postcards of Paris and defined the city for those who didn't live there. But when I reached the river, I felt overwhelmed by the thought of everything that lay ahead.

One evening, I stood watching the brown water, panic rising up my throat. I found a bench and sat down, and I thought that I would not be able to get back home because I was so tired. After a while, I got up and started walking slowly, recovering my energy. By the time I approached my neighborhood and could see the turn to my street, I was thinking that I should have walked farther, and told myself that I would explore more the following day.

Some days, I sat at the Café du Coin at the entrance to my building. I often came there at lunchtime, though I did not eat, just sipped coffee, and was ushered to a small table by the back wall. Even after several weeks, the young waiter did not seem to remember me. He asked for my order with impatience and always brought a different size coffee than I had ordered. The café regulars ate copious salads piled with meats, or a tagine served with pickles and dried fruits. Some days they had a glass of beer, other times they ended their meals with dessert. I was struck by how appropriate their choices seemed. How they managed to pick the most fitting dish for that hour of that particular day. I wondered how it was that people knew what to do. Small things, I mean. The rituals of a day. The hours.

After the waiter cleared the regulars' plates, he brought them coffee and joined them outside for a cigarette. But first he would come to my table and tap twice, meaning that he wanted to settle my bill. I sat for a few more minutes, then gulped the remains of my cup, left some coins on the table, and climbed the stairs back up to my room.

THERE IS A SCENE IN ONE OF M.'S NOVELS, SET IN ISTANBUL. I read it when I came back to take care of my mother, and read that scene again when I moved to Paris. I already knew, in those first weeks, that M. lived in Paris as well, and this seemed strange to me. I couldn't imagine him anywhere other than Istanbul, in the landscape of his lonely characters.

In the scene, an old man walks past a bakery one evening,

around sunset. It is the month of Ramadan and the bakery has a line of people waiting to buy bread before joining their families for dinner. (I forgave M. this cliché of writing about Istanbul on a Ramadan evening.) There is a long description of desserts filling up shop windows as the time for breaking fast approaches. For a second, M. seems to forget about his character and indulges in a description of mounds of shaved pistachio, rose-scented dough, and buttery pastries, like jewels that decorate the windows. It's just like him to turn away like this, to give in to the temptation of a feast in his writing. But the sentence that follows has remained with me ever since:

Seeing all the people standing in the bakery line with purpose, the old man feels embarrassed and turns away from the steaming stacks of bread on the counter.

When I first read this, I thought that the old man was embarrassed of the bread itself, and not just the people at the bakery, and I remembered this description when I came home from my walks, those first weeks in Paris.

I would sit down at the kitchen table and feel the objects of the room taking note of my brief absence and prompt return, and I was embarrassed.

4.

"Shame on you," the aunts said when they called me in London to tell me that my mother was sick.

By this, I thought that they might mean one of two things. The first, that a daughter should know without being told about her mother's illness.

The second, that I had made my mother sick.

I realized later that the aunts were using this opportunity to tell me what they thought about my living situation—far from home and with my boyfriend, Luke, whom they hadn't met. Without a care for the world, they said. For the proper way to do things.

"Nejla let you run wild. And now she keeps quiet because she doesn't want to upset you," Saniye said.

"That's the truth. But we won't let her tiptoe around you anymore."

It had never occurred to me that my mother had allowed me to run wild. I would have said that all my life, I was the one who had walked on tiptoe.

5.

n Paris, there was a Dutch boy in the program I'd enrolled in. I met him the only time I went to the university, to hand in my registration forms. We exchanged phone numbers, and we both said how much we were looking forward to the semester. The Dutch boy told me he had spent all summer reading. He named book after book in an expanding web as if he were trying to sum up the world. I nodded my head at his list.

"You and I have so much to discuss," he added when he was done, and I agreed.

He sent me a text message some days later to ask why I hadn't come to the first class. I told him I was sick and asked him to send me the readings assigned for the following week.

He invited me to a picnic on the riverbank that weekend, on one of the islands. "A couple of us from class are meeting up while the weather's still nice. You should come and cure yourself with a celebration."

I walked all the way to the river, crossed to the Île Saint-Louis, and spotted the gathering from a distance. My classmates were dressed in somber, stylish colors, holding their glasses with both hands as if they were precious objects. They all had so much curiosity on their faces as they chatted and nodded, nimbly holding their drinks, that I could not even imagine what they might be talking about. It occurred to me that I hadn't brought anything for the picnic and turned back.

On my way home, I watched a group of rollerbladers on the Pont Saint-Louis dressed in tweed suits and bowler hats, weaving in and out of plastic cones in tune to classical music. (M. would tell me later that he did not like this bridge, because it was not part of the real city; it belonged to tourists. And the two of us always walked the adjacent Pont de la Tournelle.) One of the rollerbladers, an older man who was a bit slower than the others, tipped his hat at me as he twirled around a cone.

When the Dutch boy sent another text, I told him I had enjoyed the readings and I would see him soon. After that, I mostly kept my phone turned off, except for the times I called my mother's aunts.

I told them Paris was beautiful, the true capital of the world as they liked to say.

"*Sur la rue de Rivoli, un jeune homme et une belle fille,*" the aunts chimed in chorus.

This was something they said whenever Paris came up in conversation. A line they remembered from their schoolbook.

"It just doesn't feel right," they added. "All alone over there."

I was busy with classes, I told them; I barely had a minute to myself.

6.

When I lived with my boyfriend, Luke, in London, I didn't call him by his name. I called him "Buddy" even though that's not a word from my own vocabulary. I don't know how I came to call him this, and without any irony, as if I were a native speaker of English. But then, as I said, I was building my life piece by piece and it seemed that I had started from scratch.

He called me "Buddyback."

"You're my buddy," I told him one night, and he said, "You're my buddyback."

And then that's what he called me.

"Hey, Buddyback," he said.

"Hey, Buddy," I said, when we woke up in the studio we had decorated with all the objects of our new selves: piles of psychol-

ogy books, decorations from countries we hadn't visited, little rit-
ualistic objects with which we ordered our days—incense sticks,
candles, ceramic mugs.

Luke was more advanced than I was in the piece-by-piece construction. He talked about setting boundaries, about the thresh-
olds of maturity, about healing the inner child. He told me about
his family as if opening envelopes one at a time, putting each one
aside before moving to the next. We started with his mother,
moved on to his siblings, arrived at his father.

He once made me a diagram that listed all the combinations
of adult-child-parent relationships and asked me to populate the
empty boxes with the people in my life. We used to do this sort
of thing to get to know one another. Questionnaires, mental
maps, associative drawings.

"Adult-to-adult," I wrote in the box representing our relationship.

In the box for my mother I wrote, "Adult-to-child." Then I
changed my mind and wrote, "Child-to-child."

When I first came to England for university, I had read a
rhyming children's book while visiting the home of my roommate, Molly. She told me this was her favorite book growing up
and I wished that it would have been mine, too. It was constructed from pure nonsense, full of delight at its own sounds.
More than the book, I envied the type of child Molly must have
been, and the childhood she must have had.

I bought the book when I moved in with Luke and told him

that it was one of the treasures of my own childhood. We read it aloud in bed, giggling. Luke didn't ask whether the book had rhymed in Turkish as well. And I was swept away by the pleasure of this invented intimacy.

"Buddy," I used to say. "Buddy, buddy, buddy."

7.

During my childhood, on the evenings that she did not go silently to her room, my mother would stand at my door before I went to sleep. I would have put away my books, my clothes, the bits of paper strewn about from my various projects. I would fold my socks together as my grandmother had taught me and tuck them inside a slipper before getting into bed. This was the ritual that brought each day of my childhood, after my father's death, safely to a close.

"Nunu," my mother said from the threshold.

"Nejla," I said.

Sometimes she said, "Nunito."

Sometimes she said, "Nunu, Nunito, Nukotiniko."

Other times, my mother looked at me as if trying to determine who I was. Then she came and sat at the edge of my bed.

"What a tidy room," she said. I didn't know if she meant it as praise.

On the best days and on the worst, she would say, "Let's remember our day."

"First, we had breakfast. You cut your cheese in the neatest triangles . . . On the way to the ferry we saw a yellow car, which reminded us of a turtle . . . The brass handle of the Baylan patisserie was shaped like a dolphin."

She never recounted the day's significant events, like the time we ran into her friend Robert on the ferry, or the Sunday afternoon when we left a restaurant mid-meal because of a group of men. Nor did she offer any commentary about the items on her daily catalog. But I knew that they were included for a reason. I guessed that the rusty yellow car had reminded her of the one we had when my father was alive; or that she mentioned the patisserie's brass handle to tell me in her own way that there had at least been a sweet moment during our day, despite her long silence.

"What a day," she said, to conclude. "So much to remember."

8.

Paris was full of people having meals. This is what I remember from that time. And also, the terra-cotta pots of plants squeezed side by side on the tiniest balconies. The first impression of a city is supposed to be the most authentic—the only time an outsider is allowed to see its essence. Everywhere around me, I saw life sprouting.

One time when I returned from a walk, I sat down at the Café du Coin and decided that I would have a good meal. I asked for the menu and looked at it for a long time.

I ordered tartare and I also ordered a steak. Then I asked for hot chocolate.

Only when the waiter stood looking in disbelief did I realize the incongruity of my order. He brought the tartare first, and the hot chocolate only when, out of pride, I reminded him.

When he saw that I hadn't touched the raw meat, he asked if

I still wanted the steak. I told him I did. Afterwards I asked to have the whole thing packed. I knew that wasn't a usual request in Paris. (Neither was it in Istanbul.)

"Sure," the waiter said. "You can have it for breakfast, with a cup of hot chocolate."

The box of meat sat in my refrigerator for weeks. I would open the fridge and see that nothing had changed of its outer appearance. Sometimes, sitting at the kitchen table, I looked at the fridge and was surprised that everything appeared normal. I imagined the rotting, molding meat inside and yet I saw no sign of decay, no inconvenience to my routine. Day after day, I saw that all looked well, surrounded by the box and locked in the fridge.

I don't know what it was, but I was testing something. The order of the world; its tipping point.

9.

Luke would say that people lived their whole lives telling stories, and by story he meant something like delusion. Everyone, he said, had a story of themselves. They told it again and again, at every chance they got.

It seemed like an obvious statement to me even though I never told him that. I told Luke that I had not had an easy childhood, aware that this sounded dark and exotic. My father had been a poet but had died at an early age, when I was very young. I still remembered what it was like to live with a creative mind, I said, how it hovered above us.

In reality, I had never seen my father write. He'd given it up before I could remember. I'd seen only how he retreated within himself.

I also told Luke that my mother hadn't been able to see my father for who he was. She'd wanted him to be like everyone else,

I said. She rejected his creative world, so harshly that it shattered him. That was the language Luke and I spoke. Perhaps I even felt that these words didn't quite belong to me, and so I could say anything at all. But I was aware of the itch, quietly insistent; I tried to get at it with my words.

I told Luke I'd grown up in the shadow of my mother's unhappiness. My childhood, I said coolly, had been washed away by her own sad story.

But I had come to terms with this, I said, and to support my point I used words like *self-worth* and *compassion*.

At the time, I hadn't been back to İstanbul in three years.

Luke listened gravely, nodding his head and reaching out to squeeze my shoulder from time to time. Those were exciting moments, those indulgences. I thought I could tell him anything at all.

10.

When my father was alive and we lived in Moda, my mother would take me out in the early evening for a walk. We always left in a hurry, without calling to my father to say goodbye, slamming the door behind us.

Once we were outside, we walked as quickly as we had left, past the grocer's, past the mosque, following the curving tram tracks. I would have to run to keep up with my mother. We would arrive at the Moda cape, at the hour when seagulls cried in panicked flocks, trying to ward off the sky from collapsing in deep colors. We stood silently watching the ferries in the distance. After some time, when I began to feel worried and asked to go back home, my mother might tell me about the emerald peaks of the mythical Mount Kaf, whose reflection gave the sky its hues. This mountain, she said, was very far away. It was farther than the dark sea surrounding the earth, which even the sturdiest ship could not sail, and its sole inhabitants were djinns and fairies.

It was as if she offered me this place in exchange for our own apartment, for my father sitting in the armchair.

On our way back, we sometimes saw the chestnut seller rubbing his blackened hands over the coals. Then, my mother would stop and say, "Let's have a celebration." Chestnuts, I learned, were something special, despite the ease of acquiring them, their dry taste, and the unsmiling man who sold them to us.

When we returned home, I called to my father to include him in our celebration.

"We brought you chestnuts! Come and get your chestnuts!"

I don't remember him ever responding.

"Come get them before we eat them all!"

"Your father's writing," my mother would tell me.

But my father would be in his study, sitting in the armchair by the window, softly muttering to himself. From the way he rocked back and forth, I thought that he might be cold.

"What're you saying?" my mother asked when she saw him like that. "Please stop playing games."

Sometimes she shouted.

But even I could see that my father couldn't stop himself. I felt sorry for my mother's ignorance, her childish belief that my father was pretending, like the games I played when I lay down dead and listened to life continuing in the city outside.

11.

S ome days, I could not see Paris for what it was.

Those first months, I read and reread M.'s novels. I slipped effortlessly into that world I knew so well, where insight was spared, where tragedy occurred in parentheses, and moments of great joy were subdued.

From my window, I saw pools of orange light beneath lampposts, circles of leaves on the pavement. The city changed day after day, slipping into a new season, without my taking part.

I read absently, forgetting for pages at a time what was happening, then coming to a detail so crisp—a round tray of cucumbers in a grocery store, lit by a single fluorescent bulb—that it felt like I could reach out right in front of me for my own city.

I read, morning changing to afternoon, afternoon to night, the station outside gathering and dispersing like a beating heart, the shadows looming and contracting. And my room grew bigger and dimmer with the echoes of Istanbul.

12.

After the sun had set and we returned home from our walk, my father would get up from the armchair and leave the house without a word. Our lives were like a dance—arriving and taking off. Passing each other day after day.

When he came back, it would be late, and he would have been out for a long time. We heard him, my mother and I, in our separate rooms. I knew my mother heard him, too, I can't say how. Silence is its own language.

We listened to him turn the key, close the door, stand in the hallway. Already, with those sounds, I could feel my mother's anger.

Then he came to my room. Sometimes I kept my eyes closed and pretended to sleep, letting him sit on the floor to gather his energy. Other times, I propped myself up against the pillow.

He would ask me what I wanted to see in my dream, and I told him zebras, elephants, lions.

"In that case," my father said, "we're both going on long journeys tonight."

I remember that the apartment in Moda was long and narrow, with rooms following each other like a train: the hallway, my bedroom, the kitchen, my father's study, the dining room, the television room, my parents' bedroom, the balcony. I remember it as a train, because that's what my father told me.

"Two compartments crossed," he said. "Six to go."

But in truth, the eighth and final compartment in this game—when he reached the balcony—was the reward, and didn't count. Even when he was back home, he wanted to be out again, to stand in the open air.

So I counted on my fingers and told him:

"Only five more."

The most challenging was the final compartment, through my parents' bedroom where my mother would be awake.

The eight compartments of this journey, my father said, were like the eight rooms of my full name. "I gave you this name," he used to say. "It's a present from me."

Then he started counting on his fingers: N, U, R, U, N, I, S, A.

Perhaps he was teaching me to read. I can't know for sure. This isn't a story I've ever told.

And I even wonder at this memory, unlike most others of my father. This moment of clarity.

My father said that there were two sets of paired compartments in his quest to reach the end of the train. The two *N*'s—the hallway and the dining room—were places of transition, where he would have to stop and listen before he could go on. The *U*'s—my bedroom and his study—were points of rest, where he could gather his strength.

When he was leaving my room, he said in a voice like the robots in cartoons, "Second round, complete. Next stop, *R*."

He waved at me from the door and I wished him luck. I listened to his steps, from room to room, counting along with him, holding my breath when I heard him approach the bedroom. My mother might get out of bed, then, and present an obstacle, and my father would not be able to reach the balcony.

13.

One afternoon in Paris, when I was going home from an aborted walk, I saw M.'s name in a bookshop window, announcing a reading by a group of English-language authors, unified under the title "Narratives of the City." One of the authors on the list had recently become famous for his novel about Paris's golden age, about a time when artists and writers had shared ideas and drinks. The book was immediately identifiable from its bright yellow cover—I had even seen translations of it in Istanbul—with a crowd of people sitting at a piano, a desk, or standing behind an easel, all of them dressed up for dancing. Though I had not read the novel, its subject did not seem too different from the life I had imagined for myself in Paris with Luke.

On the evening of the reading I arrived at the shop early and took a seat in front, close to a wall. M. arrived some minutes later and excused himself to the bookshop staff before taking the last chair on the small makeshift stage, directly opposite mine. Then he started leafing through his novel.

He was different from his pictures. I had not known that he was very tall and thin, and he sat hunched on the chair, as if trying to diminish his size. He was wearing a crumpled shirt and a navy-colored sweater, a bit too big for him. I'd thought he would be neatly dressed, even meticulously, perhaps because of the way he named streets one by one in his novels, listed trees, shops, and foods, building an entire world with the patience of a miniaturist.

The year I lived in Istanbul, taking care of my mother, I had read a review of M.'s last novel in a Turkish newspaper. The reviewer said that while it was a pleasure to see Istanbul through foreign eyes, it could be tiresome to look at it stone by stone. It made me happy to read this, as if I alone understood M.'s writing.

I had read in the same review that M. went regularly to one of the burger stands in Taksim Square and I would imagine what it would be like to run into him there. The reviewer questioned what it meant for a foreigner to share the rituals so dear to us, İstanbullus. (I hadn't realized until then that the burger stands were so special.) The reviewer also wondered whether the love of a Turkish woman—a painter to whom M. had been married for a short period—was enough to grant a writer access to the city. Surely, he wrote, Istanbul was much more than its sights and sounds recorded with patience, and carried like a wound by M.'s lonely character, whose withdrawal from the world was perhaps a sign of M.'s own foreignness to the city, not to mention his limited understanding of it. There was never the possibility of sharing the joys and sorrows of the character, the reviewer concluded. In the end, reading M.'s novels, despite their wealth of detail, was like walking through Istanbul on a foggy night.

As I said, the review made me happy.

In my daydream about running into M., I imagined that we would be reading the same book, while we ate standing at a counter. We'd laugh at this coincidence, start a conversation, then walk all the way down İstiklal Street, jumping from topic to topic or walking silently like old friends.

WHEN PEOPLE IN THE AUDIENCE BEGAN TAKING THEIR SEATS, M. put away his novel, which he had marked with bits of paper. A woman who was standing at the back of the room asked loudly whether this was indeed the reading about Paris. M. looked at me and smiled.

"Better leave while you still can," he said.

The famous author was the last to arrive and he came with a group of young people who might have been his students. He walked up to M. and slapped him on the back, telling the students that they were in good company.

"Forget about me," he said. "Here's the real author. You should all discover this man's brilliant writing."

M. was the last to read. Before he began, the program host asked him to describe his connection to Istanbul.

"For many of us," the host said, "Istanbul is a mythical city.

It is Constantinople, it is the fallen Rome. It's the meeting point of East and West."

He remembered his first visit to Istanbul. There had been many more visits after that, he said. One could not help falling in love with the city. He had the feeling of walking through history, through entire empires and civilizations. Several people in the audience nodded vigorously, eagerly affirming the impression of their own visits.

This was a time when Istanbul's name was popular around the world. Much was made of its diversity, the so-called meeting point of two worlds. All of a sudden, there were books upon books about Istanbul, its sad and glorious past—in these books, it seemed, Istanbul was always sad and glorious, as if the city had done nothing but decay from an unseen splendor. Even Turkish writers had begun to discover their own city with fresh eyes. That period has mostly ended, by now. Those were better times.

"How about you?" the host finally asked M. "How do you step beyond the mythical to the real city? I guess my question is, do you ever manage to do so?"

M. was silent for a moment.

"I don't want to be trite," he said. "It can sound that way when I try to articulate it."

"Alright," the host said. "So, you don't want to articulate your view of the city. What else can you tell us?"

There was laughter among the audience. M. smiled and turned to a page he had marked. He looked at it for a while.

"Actually," he said, "I think I'll read something else."

He flipped through the novel back and forth and finally read a short scene set in Moda. I remembered this scene well, about the rocky beach, and the strange evening colors of the sky.

At the end of the talk, the famous author was flocked by the audience members.

I followed M. to the back of the shop where he was talking to two elderly men about the occupation years in Istanbul. In my bag, I had two of his novels and I was waiting for the right moment to approach him. But when his conversation eventually ended, I changed my mind and pretended to browse the shelves.

It must be an illusion common to all readers who've loved a book that they are destined to be good friends with its author; that they alone understand this person and share a special bond. I knew this and still, I did not want to have the short and disappointing conversation when M. would greet me cordially, thank me for coming, and sign my book. I would tell him my full name, so that he would notice it was Turkish, unlike the ambiguous Nunu. Perhaps he would ask me a question or two, before adding a warm greeting. *To Nurunisa, with friendship.*

That year in Istanbul, I had read passages from M.'s novels to my mother. One passage, I remember, was a description of cypresses. This was another one of M.'s indulgences in writing, when he looked away from his lonely character to describe trees, as if he were painting them one by one.

"All these foreigners think Istanbul is full of cypresses," my mother said when I put the book down. "I wonder if this man ever set foot in the city."

I told her he had lived in Istanbul while writing the novel.

"Then he must be blind," she said.

I assumed my mother discredited the cypresses' reputation simply because she did not like them. When we drove to visit my grandparents in Aldere, the cypress trees around the Edirnekapı Cemetery, where my father was buried, approached like dark clouds. My mother would drive without speaking until they disappeared behind us.

14.

After my father's death, my mother sent me for a month to stay with my grandparents—her parents—in Aldere, a Thracian town some hours away from Istanbul. I was seven years old and I spent most of that time in the kitchen with my grandmother before going to school for a few hours in the afternoon. While my grandmother cooked, I lay on my back on the wooden divan, one leg crossed over the other, identifying the constellations of cracks on the ceiling. My grandmother sang along to the songs on the radio and I sang along in my head.

She asked me every day what I would like for lunch and I told her spinach pastries, baklava, toast with sour cherry jam, coffee with milk and honey. If she was making dumplings, she gave me dough to play with. If she was frying potatoes, she made stamps shaped like diamonds that I pressed into paint and printed on starched white cloths.

One evening after dinner, we sat in the garden with the town doctor and his wife, who arrived with a bag of toys that belonged to their grandchildren. That month, I was allowed to sit with the adults late into the night. I sorted through the bag, examining the neon-colored bears and kittens, and I was filled with loneliness looking at these animals that were another child's friends. I thought they were looking at me with pity and that they wanted to be free of me, so they could go back to the other child.

"As surely as the seasons," I heard one of the adults say. "He wasn't the same. He changed as surely as the seasons."

"Your heart breaks."

"But there was nothing to do. He could hardly . . ."

"Like an infant."

"It's even a relief, God forgive me."

"It wore her out, of course."

I was listening to the conversation as if in a dream, drifting along with the words. From time to time one of the adults would look in my direction and they would all begin to whisper, but after some time their voices would rise again like a tide.

"Good for nothing," my grandfather said suddenly, and he brought down his spoon on the table so loudly that we were all startled.

For many years, I pulled the words out and examined them, trying to focus very hard.

15.

These days, all anyone in Istanbul can talk about is the change. It's happening at great speed. Perhaps I shouldn't call it a change, but an unraveling. Something we were blind to until now.

There are demolitions, demonstrations, marches. There are those who disappear; who don't get to tell their story. And there is that constant, maddening hum of the city that drowns it all out, so that we lose track of all that's twisting, turning, disappearing, and appearing anew under the title of a new villain.

It's impossible to tell at this moment how any of this will settle. For the time being, we're waiting. Everyone has their opinion, of course, and each opinion is as fearful as the other.

But I want to record one thing, in the midst of everything: the old establishments—shops, restaurants, teahouses, and patisseries known to us by name, as the city's landmarks—are closing one by one. Their buildings are torn down to be replaced with others; brand-new signs take the place of their worn-out names, which we never bothered to look at, as familiar they were to us as our own names.

And there are the cinemas, of course, and the theaters—Emek Sineması, Lale Sineması, Şan Tiyatrosu.

When my parents were at university, the aunts told me, my father would wait for my mother at the Kanlıca plaza to take her to the Emek Cinema. Those must have been the years of the Godfather movies, but that's my own guess. I imagine they would arrive at the Kabataş port, and walk the back streets of Tarlabaşı, not minding the catcalls of cross-dressers lining the sidewalks, mustachioed men patrolling the steep streets, the neon light seeping out of brothels, coffeehouses bustling with neighborhood drama.

And who knows, the two of them might have bought chestnuts when they finally emerged onto İstiklal Street.

"He would drop from the sky," the aunts said, telling the story of my father waiting at the plaza with his notebook until my mother came down.

"That's how he did it. He just waited around until she gave in."

It would snow and it would rain and my father continued to wait, bent over his notebook. This was a different story of my father's strange ways, when they could still be contained in anecdotes.

"That poor boy," Saniye sometimes said. And with those words, my father would change. His strange ways, once so innocent, would suddenly take on new meaning.

ISTANBUL WAS ONCE AN INNOCENT PLACE, WITH ALL ITS TRUST-worthy names. But those names are mostly gone.

There is a fear of time passing. And everywhere the signs of age are eradicated.

16.

nother one of Luke's theories was that every relationship consisting of two people had a third leg. In the time that we lived together, his theories would sweep our life like a flood, washing everything in their colors.

Luke showed me, moving his fingers along invisible planes, how the unstable structure looked with two and three foundations. I thought that he was talking about the two of us (and that our third point of support was the stories we told each other about our families), but he continued with his theory: that my mother had recruited me as the third point of support in her relationship with my father.

We were sitting on our bed, covered with a paisley quilt. It was a dark place, that room, like a den, or the inside of someone's head.

"Your mother needed you to be on her side," he said. "She

took you away from him because you were compassionate. But the moment you stopped participating . . . ," he said.

He leaned over to hold my hand.

AT THE TIME, I DIDN'T KNOW WHAT SORT OF DAMAGE COULD be caused with words. I didn't know, either, what would be lost.

17.

When my mother and I moved from Moda to the new apartment, we started playing the silence game. We started it right after I came back from my grandparents' in Aldere.

I had imagined that when I was back and the two of us were finally alone, my mother would explain what had happened to us. I continued to wait for her explanation for years, even as I established the rules of our shared silence.

I would come home from school and slide the key into the lock, turning it with care. Inside, I unstrapped my shoes, slowly, like pulling at cloth stuck to a scar. I followed the trail of rugs to my room and changed out of my school clothes. I would either sit down to do my homework, or lie on my bed reading a book, listening to my mother's sounds in the apartment.

My mother would be at her desk or in the kitchen making dinner. After I went to my room, I heard the sound of water from the shower, and I gave myself several points in the game. When there was no danger of my mother hearing me, I would take things out of my schoolbag, or go to the kitchen for a snack. There would always be something for me on the table— a plate of fruits, peeled and sliced, or a glass of milk and walnut cookies.

Once she was out of the shower, my mother called to me from her bedroom, asking why I hadn't come in to say hello.

"Just a minute, Nejla," I called back, to give her some more time alone.

After breakfast on Saturdays, if my mother brought her book to read at the table without clearing the dishes, I would say that I just needed to get something from my room and would slip out. The trick was to ease her into our routine, without her having to tell me. Otherwise the game would be over.

As far as I can remember, it had happened only once or twice that I lost so suddenly, when my mother asked me directly if I would please leave her alone.

On good days, when I collected points smoothly, the breakfast dishes remained on the table, and I left them there just as my mother had. If she saw or heard me around the house, she would come and talk to me, or ask if I was hungry. She asked kindly, like an apology. When this happened, I lost several points.

I told my mother I was working on something in my room

and had to get back to it. In this game, I was the one who needed solitude.

"I hope you won't want to be all by yourself tomorrow," my mother said. "It's the day for our walk."

Such statements from my mother, when she played along, won me double points.

If we passed a whole day in silence in our separate rooms, I announced myself the winner and waited for my reward in the evenings, when my mother came to the doorway.

"Nunu, Nunito, Nukotiniko."

DURING THOSE DAYS WHEN I COLLECTED POINTS WITH EACH passing hour, I built my paper city. I had a stack of my mother's newspapers—the small-print, leftist *Cumhuriyet* I used for building walls; the colorful *Hürriyet*, full of shocking stories about centenarians and talking animals, I used to construct telephone poles; and the thick black letters of *Milliyet* I used to pave my labyrinthine streets. The city twisted and turned around itself, with courtyards and dead ends that I alone could see from my godly vantage point but that were invisible to the people walking its streets.

My city did not resemble Istanbul, except that it had two shores, separated by bridges. The boardwalk was dotted with benches that I populated with my paper citizens, letting them watch the city of which they knew so little. Sometimes, feeling sorry for their pathetic vision, I granted them entry into a

courtyard, or took them on a walk around my mazelike neighborhoods. Or I walked them along the train tracks I had built
without destination.

My favorite citizens were the unfortunate clay and newspaper amputees whose arms and legs had come off, whose small
heads and smudged newspaper faces saddened me. For them,
I organized special walking tours—with red pieces of thread
around their waists—when I gave them powers to walk verti-
cally, defying gravity, while all the others watched, collected at
the boardwalk. With my help, these quiet people, who had never
complained to me of their amputated states, pattered up bridges
and telephone poles, twirling with joy when they reached the
highest points.

The headlines of my childhood were all folded inside the
paper city. The northern side was built with the names of army
generals, the IRA, Bosnia, Yugoslavia, PKK. To the south, my
construction of an amusement park coincided with the building of the dam in Southeast Anatolia. The words that confused
me, that seemed to have a life of their own—*inflation*, *coalition*,
constitution—were neatly rolled up to serve as pipes and chim-
neys for buildings. I reconstructed the city frequently, rebuild-
ing courtyards and opening up dead ends, adding current news
on top of older news.

One afternoon, as I was laying down the foundations for a
new district, I saw a story about a group of young girls in an
eastern village who had committed suicide. At first, I did not read
the entire headline, but saw only the word, as if it had reached out

from the paper and struck me across the face. I was so startled that I turned the paper around. I had never seen this word in writing; I was only aware that it hovered above, its name barely uttered. Only one time in Aldere, and once when the aunts were talking to a neighbor woman. Spoken in a strange whisper that I wondered whether I had heard correctly.

I got up and closed the door to my room.

The newspaper wrote that this, this word, was the girls' only relief in their oppressive lives. Still, I didn't really understand the story. I couldn't make sense of the threat that faced the girls, nor did I know why the newspaper wrote that they had escaped to their freedom, as if they had triumphed.

I folded up the page several times and used it to pave the narrow road that led from my city's busiest neighborhood to the outskirts, where I built a walled-off garden. Over time, I decided to repave the road, and covered it with a densely scripted page from *Cumhuriyet*.

My own house was inside this garden, and the bright tubes of newspaper coupons were the trees I saw from my bedroom window. In the winter, I covered the trees with patches of cotton.

The newspaper house itself, where I lived with my mother, was wide and low, like my grandparents' house in Aldere. I built houses for the aunts and for my grandparents as well. They all lived close to each other but at a distance from our house, so that my mother did not have to see them all the time.

There was also a path leading to an opening in the garden wall and past it, through the opening, to a small cabin.

On afternoons when I had collected enough points and was certain that my mother was immersed in her world, I would allow one of my favorite citizens to visit this cabin where, unknown to anyone but the two of us, my father continued to live.

18.

After the reading in the bookshop, several of the writers and some people from the audience gathered at the front of the shop, discussing the best of four restaurants in the neighborhood.

"Now that we're out," the famous author said, "we might as well go all out. I rarely do this type of thing."

"Here's a piece of advice," he said to the young girl standing next to him. "Don't become a writer if you want to live an interesting life."

He asked M. whether he would join them. M. said he was too tired and that he hoped they would have a wonderful time.

"That's what I mean," the famous author said, and the girl laughed.

After they left, M. stayed at the shop for a few more minutes.

I was browsing a shelf of poetry books and I heard him tell the shop owner that he was working on a new book. It was set in Turkey, once again, but this time in a small town close to Istanbul.

"We should schedule a reading to hear the work in progress," the shopkeeper said.

"Well," M. said, "no progress yet. I'm still nosing around."

I left the shop after him, walking a few steps behind before I caught up to tell him that I had enjoyed the reading, especially his passage about Istanbul.

"My hometown," I said. This sounded strange, as if Istanbul was a faraway place I could not return to.

"But you forgot one thing," I added, and told him that Moda Street did not run down uninterrupted to the water as he had described in that scene. There was also the fish restaurant.

"I kept that one to myself," M. said. "That's my spot."

Then he asked, "Have you ever had their sardines grilled in vine leaves?"

I was surprised at the ease with which M. settled into this conversation, no different from the way he veered into a list of foods in his writing. We talked for several minutes about the dishes on their menu.

When we reached the Seine, M. asked where I was headed and I pointed straight ahead, even though I was moving away from home.

"Well, then," he said, "lucky me."

We crossed the bridge to the island, mostly empty except for a few tourists in front of an ice-cream shop, then the Pont de la

Tournelle to the Left Bank, standing a moment to look at Notre-Dame glowing with a strange light through the mist. M. asked what I was doing in Paris and I told him the answer I had already prepared—that I had come there to write.

"An İstanbullu, a colleague, and a kindred appetite," M. said. "Don't tell me you're Catholic as well."

"Don't worry," I said. "I'm not your double come to haunt you."

M. laughed—a loud, generous laugh.

"The evening's taken a delightful turn," he said.

We continued up a narrow street with art galleries and a monastic bookshop. Behind the forged iron gates, courtyards were crowded with the shadows of plants, fountains, rows of bicycles. This was the city I had imagined all along, and the one I had been trying to get to in those first weeks.

After we crossed the boulevard Saint-Germain, we continued up to the Panthéon. I was seeing it for the first time and I contained my amazement at its size. A group of teenagers sat in a circle with bottles of wine, their silhouettes swallowed by the giant pillars behind them.

M. was telling me about one of his neighbors, from when he lived in Istanbul. This man owned a newspaper stand and would look up from his book and wave whenever M. walked by. It was one of the most cherished rituals of his Istanbul life.

This neighbor was the one who told M. about the fish restaurant in Moda. The two of them had even gone there together one time, though M. had never managed to become his friend.

"He was a solitary person," M. said, "but maybe that wasn't

the issue." He added that his Turkish was too rudimentary to form a meaningful friendship, even if he had always wanted to know more about him. And the stand owner didn't speak any English.

He told me he had recently heard of the neighbor's death.

"You know," he said, "I wanted to share this with someone from Istanbul. I don't know what his death would mean to just anyone. That's what I was thinking about at the reading, when I was asked that question of the mythical city.

"Do you see what I mean?" he continued. "It was a silly question, of course. But if I were to respond to it, I'd say that you cross the threshold of myth with such people. Their passing means something about that place, it shows you that the city is not immutable."

For a moment, I thought that we were talking about my mother. Throughout my friendship with M., I felt that he said things in roundabout ways, as if he were telling me that he knew something. I cannot say what he knew, only that I was uneasy under this piercing gaze. Of course, it's possible that time has added meaning to memory.

We had made a circle around the plaza and were back at the pillars.

"But I'm talking in circles," he said. "I'm not a very good guide."

We talked timidly and with enthusiasm. But without exaggeration. And there was a moment, once we crossed the river to the Left Bank—or maybe it happened earlier, when we stood on the bridge looking at the cathedral—that things were settled: M. didn't ask again where I was headed, and I didn't apologize for taking his time as I had planned on doing when we first started walking.

As we were going down from the Panthéon back towards the river, we paused in front of a café. I can't remember which one of us suggested that we should sit down for a drink. This, too, was settled without unnecessary explanations. We took a table on the terrace. When the waiter came with the menu, M. waved his hand and asked for two glasses of wine without consulting me, as if he did not want to pause our conversation.

We continued sitting at the café for some time after we finished our wines. Then, I asked M. whether he would join me for another glass.

"I was hoping you had that spirit," he said.

I don't remember them all, but there were many things he said during our friendship that made me happy.

19.

When I found out about my mother's illness and returned to Istanbul, I received an e-mail from Luke. He wished me strength in the months ahead. He considered it admirable that I was back with my mother, despite everything.

"Your every move is selfless," he wrote.

He added that I should make sure to take care of myself.

"Don't just think of others, Buddyback. Know that it's important to be kind to yourself."

"Luke," I wrote back. "I don't think you understand what's happening."

I already knew then that I would not see him again. Perhaps I'd felt all along, even when I lived with him, that I was passing the time, that my life hinged on the single moment when I'd learn that my mother was dying. Then I would set everything else aside.

Luke wrote again, some weeks later. By that time, he must have realized I wasn't coming back and he must have been angry.

He told me he could understand why I was hiding from him; because he alone knew the honest truth.

And the honest truth, he continued, was that I'd succumbed to my mother's wishes once again; I let her dictate my life. It seemed that he was suggesting my mother had lured me back with her sickness.

All he'd ever wanted, Luke wrote, was to help me heal my wounds. But he couldn't do that when I continued to live without confronting my mother.

"You mustn't let her crush you," he said. "All your life, she's made you feel guilty. Because she couldn't bear her own guilt. She's never been accountable for your father. She pushed a helpless man to the edge of despair.

"And now she wants you to tell her that all is forgiven," Luke wrote. I didn't hear from him again.

Everyone, he'd concluded, had to live and die with their own failures.

20.

When we were at the fishmonger or buying flowers, my mother would list the names of everything she saw. She was not trying to teach me, but simply honoring the sights with their proper titles. *Mullet, sardine, sea bass*, she said. *Tulip, hyacinth, anemone.* Some flowers had their colloquial names, like a type of clover that was called *lady buttons* in Aldere, where she had grown up.

In these moments, it seemed impossible that my mother's mood would darken. The world would be crisp with color, its every line easy to identify. It seemed that my mother knew the name of everything in the world, unlike the days when she was silent and the hours blurred from one to the other. We lived in a sort of cloud then.

But whenever my mother made her lists, the cloud lifted and I gained points in the game.

Sometimes, she would say one of her strange words and I wondered whether she did not live in two places at the same time. The word that comes to me now is *kukuleta*, which, the first time I heard it, sounded like a birdsong. I was sick in bed and my mother was showing me pictures from her childhood in Aldere. She pointed at herself wearing a hooded cape, among a group of men coming back from hunting.

"Look at me with my *kukuleta*," she said, and she laughed, though it seemed that this was a private laughter, meant for herself. These were the moments when I could see the glittering remains of a person I had never known.

21.

After our drinks on boulevard Saint-Michel, M. and I walked back to the river, this time crossing at Pont Neuf, then walked all the way up to Gare du Nord. I parted with him some streets away from where I lived. I didn't want him to see my building, whose entrance after sunset was often occupied by women waiting for customers.

"This was wonderful," M. said, and I wondered whether I should give him a hug, or kiss him on both cheeks. But he took his hand out of his coat pocket and raised it in the air for a moment, before putting it back and walking away.

The next morning, he wrote me an e-mail to tell me that we had forgotten to list one of the specialties at Moda's fish restaurant—smoked bonito with sun-dried tomatoes. But more importantly, he added, he hoped that I would indulge him with more stories. I haven't forgotten this word, *indulge*.

I did not see him again for several weeks, during which time we delved deep into a correspondence in writing. "An indulgence," as he called it once again. This, too, was settled like our first walk, with no pretense at formality, without excuse or apology.

After the first time, M. would write to me midsentence— "Listen to this," he began, or, "You're mistaken." He wrote as if he were sitting across the table from me and our conversation of the first evening had not ended. This is the person I knew best, this voice who spoke to me across the city, as if he were looking me straight in the eyes.

But by the time I saw him again, I knew little more about M. than I did during our first walk. It seemed that instead of covering long distances, we were digging deeper with our heels on a dirt track.

M. had a way of circumventing practicalities. He would write things like, "If it weren't for the daily tasks that take over my day, I would devote my attention to my new book, my Thracian project, set close to your mother's beautiful Aldere, which you describe so poetically." But he did not explain what these "daily tasks" were. Instead, he wrote to say how lucky it was that he had met me now, at a time when he was searching for a guide into the landscapes of Thrace.

One time he referred to Paris as a "sad and forgiving city" and I did not ask him why he thought this. I felt that this sort of curiosity for facts would betray the rules of our correspondence. This is also why I didn't refer to anything outside our friendship— all the things I had previously known about him—and M. did not bring them up. I did not mention, either, that I had read his novels.

As I said, I felt that all the rules of our friendship were settled unspoken, and I realize now that they were peculiarly similar to what I would have wanted them to be had we determined them outright. In my childhood and even later, I had dreamed of having such a friend with whom I could exchange endlessly on strange topics of my choosing, without the worry of stepping into uncomfortable territory.

At the time, I thought that *indulgence* was a word from M.'s own vocabulary and way of life, but now I think that perhaps he was naming something he observed in me.

22.

My mother grew up in Aldere walking in a forest with Akif amca, Uncle Akif, the next-door neighbor. This was the story she told most often, and she always started it just like this:

"I grew up walking in a forest with Akif amca."

It's how she wanted me to know her, and she insisted on telling it this way, as if the years had passed and she grew older and taller without stepping out of that forest. On the best days, on the very best I mean, when I forgot about my game because the points piled up effortlessly, she would come to my room and she would have no reason to recount our day, to create it from scratch. Instead, she told me about Aldere. And insofar as memories and stories are interchangeable once enough time has passed, this is the story of my childhood as well.

At that time, the town's sugar factory brought Aldere to life in the months when trucks, piled with beets, drove in from all around the region. They would slow down as they entered the curving road, heftily shifting gears by my grandparents' yellow house at the town's edge.

My mother was among the first of the town's children to follow the trucks all the way to the factory gate, collecting the beets that fell on the road. Some children sold their modest harvest to the factory for a few kuruş—enough for a scoop of ice cream, or, if the truck had taken the curve too fast, spilling beets into the roadside ditch, a hand fan or a pack of cards from my grandfather's shop. Some children would take the beets home to roast on coals. My mother carried hers to Akif amca's garden, and balanced them on the mouths of glass bottles. Akif amca would bring out a rifle from the woodshed and watch, nodding his head, as she shot them one by one.

During its months of activity, when the air was thick with the smell of molasses, the factory hosted concerts, game nights, and lunches for Aldere's wealthy families. But the season's crowning event was the Sugar Ball, when the town women were taken by panic, unstitching old taffeta dresses to put together new models from sewing catalogs, in their best imitation of Istanbul's high society. Invitations to these events—one of which my mother and I found during our last trip to Aldere, still in its handwritten envelope—kindly asked that no children be brought. My mother spent those evenings with Akif amca, even if my grandmother otherwise thought that he was an inappropriate influence.

Akif amca had moved to Aldere when my mother was born, to

work as a manager at the factory. He never attended the town's events, and after a few years, he was no longer invited. Besides, the townspeople grew suspicious of this man with a foreigner's manners, whose voice became louder with the glasses of raki he drank while sitting in his garden, when he began to tell his visitors, or whoever happened to be passing by, his outrageous stories. The neighbors smiled politely at the mention of places he claimed to know intimately—Rome, London, Madrid, Paris. Older boys on their way home from school shouted out in a mock drunken singsong when they passed the overgrown garden, "I'm walking down the *Shanzelizeee!*"

More suspicious still was Akif amca's houseful of books and papers, unlike the neat homes of Aldere's elite, which were crystalled and porcelained by the factories of Europe—Limoges, Prague, Meissen. These place-names were not floating like Akif amca's fantastic stories, but were stamped on sugar bowls, coffee trays, and thumb-sized villager girls carrying milk pails. They filled the households indisputably with European respectability.

My mother's stories of the walks started with the sound of her parents' exit from the wrought-iron gate, braided with roses. She would jump over the wall to Akif amca's garden and wait for him to fetch his walking stick from the shed. Badem, the English setter, would already be at the gate, and the three of them set off for the forest in the last and golden light.

Instead of taking the main road, they walked along the creek and crossed the stone bridge, where, according to town legend, a traveler had once stood at sunset, watching the water dappled in burning colors, and had given Aldere its poetic name, "Crimson creek." (I knew all the landmarks along this walk and looked out for them in my mother's stories.)

When they passed the sunflower fields, Akif amca stopped to cut a flower with his penknife, and they picked the seeds from its wide, black tray. My mother always offered some to Badem, who sniffed politely, before running ahead.

Once inside the forest, Akif amca began his list. Chestnut, linden, pine, beech. Poppy, wood rose, dandelion. As he named the forest—for my mother an entire world—shapes emerged distinctly from the pointing tip of Akif amca's stick. Stems were thick and thin, weedy, milky, hollow. Bark was smooth, rough, or mossy. Leaves were round, leaves were sharp. They floated or fluttered, they fell spinning to the ground.

I SPENT EVERY SUMMER OF MY CHILDHOOD AT MY GRANDPARents' yellow house in Aldere. In the afternoons, I lay under the mulberry tree, looking at the stone house across the low wall that separated my grandmother's rose garden from a forest of weeds and glass bottles.

I had been inside Akif amca's house only once, one hot afternoon when my mother came to take me back to Istanbul. I remember the smell of old skin and cologne, and the eyes that watched me from the sofa.

My mother had asked me to kiss the old man's hand and present him with a box of candied chestnuts. After lunch—he insisted that we stay, and my mother, despite my silent pleas, accepted—he disappeared to the bedroom and came back with a box of objects. To my dismay, the box contained nothing but a rusty penknife, a walking stick, and some photographs.

When we were leaving, the old man told me that I had my mother's eyes.

I was used to being told that I had my father's eyes. Relatives said it with pity or fright, as if seeing a ghost.

"Look at those eyes," they said. "Just like her father's."

But Akif amca spoke with an authority that upset me, as if he were stealing what was rightfully mine—this link to my father.

"You have your mother's eyes," he said. "And are you stubborn like her as well?"

IN MY CHILDHOOD, ALDERE WAS ALREADY PAST THE DAYS OF the factory's Sugar Balls and taffeta dresses. The modest flavor of European civilization had dispersed like mist. Later, when the factory shut down for good and the houses were abandoned, I examined the black-and-white photographs of Aldere's golden age. In their shadows, I identified the vanished town I had glimpsed as a child—its tables set in crystal, its modest fur coats, its hats and walking sticks, its wrought-iron gate, and its curving road that led past the lethargic summer afternoons of my childhood to another, brighter town, its creek dappled crimson at sunset.

23.

Those first weeks, when I wrote to M. often and with enthusiasm, I went on many walks around the city, to make up for everything I had not seen when I arrived. I would come back to the studio with a list of things I wanted to tell him. To be sure, this was a short period, those few weeks of writing, but I remember it as a season of its own.

Just as he talked about the dishes in Moda's fish restaurant, M. wrote to me about the smallest details as if they were what occupied his mind above all else.

We had a long discussion about bird nests, their miraculous, compact structure, and the disappointment of seeing them come apart in mud and twigs. M. told me about a collection of birds' eggs he had as a child, listing the colors one by one, each a shade darker than the other: *wet sand, cherry bark, evening blue*, he wrote, and I marveled at his precision. I was happy that I was the recipient of this list, as if it were a poem. In return, I told him about my mother's photographs of the doorstep in Aldere, taken in varying lights, always with the broomstick against the wall. I described all the different hours of the town, which, in my telling, became more mythical still than my mother's Aldere: the misty, cold mornings, bright afternoons, woodsmoke dusks. This was how we stepped from one topic to the next, in our particular logic, without attachment to the cumbersome rationality at ground level.

M. reported on the Judas tree in his apartment building's courtyard, documenting its bare branches and anticipating its earliest buds. One time, he wrote that Judas trees always reminded him of Istanbul.

I told him that my mother had loved these trees, and that she and I used to go to the Adile Sultan Pavilion once every year for lunch to see them.

I had written to M. about my mother's passing, and he accepted the information without comment, which I interpreted as gentleness. As I said, it seemed that he already knew certain things, and I was relieved that I did not have to explain any further. But I also worried that he noticed things about me, in moments when I let my guard down.

"You haven't told me what you ate on these lunches at the Adile Sultan Pavilion," M. wrote back. I remember his impatience, his eagerness for such details.

I told him pureed fava beans, artichokes, white asparagus from İzmir, roasted lamb with thyme.

And then there were our Sunday fish lunches, I said. Those were a world to themselves.

24.

After we moved to the new apartment, my mother and I would walk along the water to Yeniköy on Sundays to have fish at Aleko's. I can't remember how this became a tradition but it must have started as one of my mother's celebrations following a long silence—those days when I collected many points in my game—after which my mother would appear at my door as if nothing had happened.

"Nunito? What are you doing here all by yourself?"

With these final, decisive points added to my score, I would look up casually from my newspaper city and shrug.

"I hope you haven't forgotten that tomorrow is the day for our walk," she said. In this story we silently agreed on, I was the one who kept forgetting, who demanded solitude.

———

ONCE WE REACHED THE BOARDWALK, WHICH STRETCHED FOR miles ahead, my mother walked faster, and I thought that she might even start running, as if she wanted to dive right into the heart of the Bosphorus. My hand in my mother's, I felt that we were seeing through a single pair of eyes, noticing the same beautiful sights, looking forward to landmarks as we walked: the three old houses on a canal in Arnavutköy, like three wizened sisters; the lines of fishermen in Bebek with their buckets of fluttering fish; the looming Rumeli fortress on the hills. Every time we approached the fortress, my mother asked me who had built it, and I quickly answered, "Mehmed the Second, 1452!"

At the threshold of each neighborhood, I announced the destination ahead, like a tour guide: "We have arrived in Emirgan. Next stop, İstinye!" Sometimes, I listed the neighborhoods of the Bosphorus in rapid succession, like reciting a nursery rhyme, taking pleasure in the names: "Ortaköy, Kuruçeşme, Arnavutköy, Bebek, Rumeli Hisarı, Baltalimanı, Emirgan, İstinye, Yeniköy, Tarabya, Kireçburnu, Büyükdere, Sarıyer." (When I lived in Paris, I repeated the stations on the metro Line 4 to myself—Saint-Placide, Saint-Sulpice, Saint-Germain-des-Prés, Odéon, Saint-Michel—with the same satisfaction.)

On some walks, my mother said, "Nunito, let's see if you can list them backwards," and I was filled with excitement. (I always gained a few points if she offered me this challenge.) I started slowly, this time using mental pictures, retracing my path from the hills of Sarıyer, past the mansions of Büyükdere to the steep and narrow road in Kireçburnu leading up from the boardwalk, which reminded me, with its overgrown garden gates, of Aldere. Walking past this road, I had the disorienting feeling that if I were to follow it, I would find my grandparents in the garden, polishing rifles or sweeping the doorstep.

Sometimes, we sat on a bench in front of the İstinye state hospital, listening to the echoes of hammers ringing from the shipyard. This tiny bay, cupping the blue-green water and crowded with lumber, ropes, and cranes, was proof for me of Istanbul's arrogant beauty. I thought that if the city could spare such a bay to a chaotic shipyard, it must have many more beautiful sights. At such moments, Istanbul split into the city I could see and a hidden city reserved for other people.

When we arrived in Yeniköy, my mother walked with her head down, past İskele Restaurant and the young waiter Yaşar waiting at the door. We had stopped going to İskele when they served us bad fish two weeks in a row, but my mother continued to feel guilty when she walked past the waiters, whom she knew by name. We hurried down the leafy road to our destination. In this last stretch of our walk, I let myself complain once.

"Nejla!" I said, dragging my feet and whining that I was tired, only to hear my mother's praise, which won me ten points, and made me champion so early in the day. There weren't many other occasions when this could happen:

"Nunito," my mother said, "you walked like a real explorer."

———

ALTHOUGH WE SWITCHED FROM İSKELE RESTAURANT TO ALEKO'S when I was ten or eleven, I always thought of it as the "new" restaurant and never took a liking to the fawning owner, Selim Bey, who called me princess and extended his clammy hand for me to climb the single step at the entrance. He led us past the corridor of glass refrigerators displaying the smiling heads of the day's catch and up the stairs to the terrace, where we sat at the back table overlooking the sea.

My mother asked Selim Bey for his recommendations, maneuvering his suggestions and ending with a plea to prepare whatever was freshest.

Selim Bey invariably answered that everything was fresh, and added, pouting, that he would not think to serve us anything else. Then he proposed a simple grilled bluefish, along with something fried, to taste, and a bit of stewed mullet as well.

"Is it the season for bluefish?" my mother worried. "Wouldn't mullet be too dry?"

My favorite was fried *istavrit*, which we ate only once or twice in early autumn. I associated the short season with the fish's tiny, glimmering body, which, I imagined, usually managed to escape even the most cunning fishing nets. On these long-awaited *istavrit* lunches, my mother told Selim Bey that we would skip appetizers and just eat fish.

Otherwise, we started with dishes chosen from the colorful tray brought to our table. My mother pointed at the aubergine salad and the white beans. She picked the feta ("Do you still get your cheese from Kardeşler?"). She might reluctantly accept the melon plate as well, even though she liked to say that melons no longer tasted as they did in her childhood.

Once our food arrived, my mother began her quiz. She tested me on the different names for bluefish, from smallest to largest (*çinekop, sarıkanat, lüfer* . . .) or asked me why there was no bonito in the Bosphorus during bluefish season. Remembering the grinning mouths in the glass fridge, I replied that the bluefish's tiny sawlike teeth would rip the bonito to smithereens.

After lunch, while my mother drank her coffee and smoked, we sat in silence, listening to the lapping of the water beneath us and the solemn call of foghorns from the ferry traveling past Yeniköy to the mouth of the Bosphorus, where the strait opened up to the sea and our prized Sunday fish swam into the nets of fishermen.

Some afternoons, if there was a table of men sitting on the terrace, my mother did not drink her coffee but asked immediately for the check (which Selim Bey presented with a stooping bow and a fan of wet towels). Once or twice, these men had raised their glasses to my mother and even sent a platter of fruit to our table, which my mother refused with a hurried smile. On those days, our lunch ended abruptly, and my mother would put my coat on me, even though I was capable of such a simple task. She insisted on pulling the zipper all the way to my neck and would yank at the sleeves without purpose, as if trying to bundle me away.

Afterwards, standing by the water, we would decide what to

do next. My mother said that it was still so early, and suggested visiting her aunts, knowing well that I would rather not. I didn't mind visiting them; I might even have enjoyed it, but my mother wouldn't be the same around them and our shared day would be over. Sometimes she offered me a story to ease the disappointment of returning home.

"Did I ever tell you about the time Akif amca went to Paris?"

But even if we didn't return just then, I knew that our outing would inevitably end and we would have to return to our regular lives, where points accumulated so slowly.

25.

omething else I told M. during that time, those weeks that
were suspended from earthly logic, was that I was writing
a novel about Akif amca. I was surprised that the idea for
the novel came to me so easily. I told him that I was tracing the
course of Akif amca's life from Istanbul to Paris and from there
back to Aldere, using his poems and the fragments from his
journals.

It's true that Akif amca had written some poems, in a journal
he kept when he was young. My mother had found the journal
on our last trip to Aldere to clean out my grandparents' house,
inside a box that also contained photographs, invitations, and
a telephone book. She kept Akif amca's journal by her bedside
in Istanbul, even though I don't remember her reading it. I had
brought it with me to Paris, not because I was hoping to discover

something in its pages—that is the stuff of novels—but to retain something of my mother's world.

"How fortunate that we ran into each other at such a time, both of us assembling our Thracian projects," M. wrote. He was neither incredulous nor dismissive and I was surprised to read that he thought of our meeting as a chance encounter.

He asked me to tell him more about my novel, if I didn't mind.

"I know how frail these ideas can be, how the landscape you are cautiously approaching can disappear behind shadows with a single false step."

I was grateful to him for including me so swiftly into his community of writers, and all the sensitivities of his profession of which I was mostly unaware.

I told M. that my novel was, like his own book, a reconstruction of a vanished world. Even if the statement was new to me, I can't say that it was a lie. What I would have liked to say was that I could write this novel with M. as my audience. That would have been the truth.

Perhaps I told him I was writing a novel about Akif amca out of pride, to make something more of my days, which by then were shaped largely around our conversations.

Every morning, I left my studio for the Saint-Quentin covered market, for a walk down to the river, or to the Passage Brady with its wealth of spice shops. I wrote to M. about these places as if they were part of my own routine, as if I had lived this way even before I met him—"This morning as I was headed to the

Italian stall at the market . . ."; "I stopped by the flower shop and the owner was as grumpy as ever."

M. told me that the simplest routines of my day were poetic. And with his observation, I tried to add more poetry to my days.

(It pains me a little to remember this now, I can't say why, but I had bought a bowl for the studio. A deep, dark blue bowl that I filled with fruits. A poetic sight, perhaps only so that I could write about it to M.)

In the afternoons, I chose specific destinations from Akif amca's journals—the old crystal factory on the rue de Paradis, the calm and leafy stretch of *péniches* on the canal Saint-Martin, the cave behind the waterfall at Parc des Buttes-Chaumont— always with a vague idea that these places might eventually fit into my imagined novel. And always, I came home to write to M. about my discoveries

AKIF AMCA'S JOURNAL CONTAINED TRAVEL NOTES, LINES COP-ied from books, and several poems. The poems were full of nostalgia for Istanbul. I found them amateurish and even didactic whenever they listed historical facts about the city, but I liked them precisely for this reason—for their naïve eagerness. But I didn't share my observations with M. I pretended that Akif amca had been a great poet, and that I now had the responsibility of bringing his work to light.

I told him about a poem whose title, "The Invention of Midnight," intrigued me. It was a mysterious title, M. agreed, and said it was a shame his Turkish was not good enough to read poetry.

He was always apologizing, I remember, but this only added to his gentle authority.

"I'm sorry for my clumsy curiosity," he wrote. "But I would be grateful if you translated this poem."

The poem itself did not live up to its title and I never translated it. It was not about a fantastical night as its name suggested, but about the literal setting of the Turkish Republic's public clocks, with the switch to the Western calendar.

But with time, the title of the poem became a code word for us, entirely different from the poem itself, and we would say the word *midnight* always with a shared understanding.

This is what I mean when I say that I was not lying. It seemed that with M. as my audience, an entire landscape of words and images emerged harmoniously, with its own particular meaning.

26.

When strangers asked us about my father, my mother told them he had been a poet. I pretended not to listen so she wouldn't be embarrassed.

"And your husband, what did he do?"

"He was a poet."

She said it without flinching.

It was the simplest story to tell about my father, and as I grew up I began to yearn for this poet with his vivid imagination. Even if all that remained of him were the two slim collections he'd written long before, which I never read. Even if, for as long as I can remember, he had no way of expressing himself, except for those moments of clarity when he came to my room and spelled my name.

"N, U, R, U, N, I, S, A."

He looked at me as if the whole world was united within a single web. As if he finally understood something.

"I gave you this name," he told me. "It's a present."

Some nights, he could not spell correctly and I had to help him with the letters.

THE MOMENTARY SILENCE THAT FOLLOWED MY MOTHER'S WORDS, when she told strangers the simple story of my father, was our own secret—our shame.

27.

My mother had heard the myth told in school that girls became boys and boys became girls when they walked under a rainbow. On their drives to Istanbul through miles of sunflower fields, when the sky revealed its arch, my mother pleaded with her father to go faster, imagining all that she would do once she crossed to the other side. She could be just like Akif amca, the way he could take his walking stick and leave, without having to account for his departure.

My mother insisted on this story of wanting to be a man. It would make me sad to hear it, but I didn't tell her. Every time she repeated the story of the rainbow, I thought she was telling me that she and I were very different, but I can't say whether she did this out of cruelty or protection.

"You had a good time, didn't you, Nunu?" she asked after visits to the aunts, which was more a statement than a question.

It was proof that I, unlike my mother, had the strange ability of enjoying the company of women.

One afternoon when we were going home, I told her about a recipe I had learned from Asuman's neighbor, who'd come over for tea and brought a cake. I explained how the swirl of color in the cake's center was achieved.

"I'll make it for you," I said.

"Oh, Nunu," my mother said. "I can't believe you fill your mind with all of this."

Around other women, my mother became a different person. When the aunts came over, she seemed to make an effort to look disheveled. She would wear a purple shirt blotched with bleach, an oversized skirt. She let her long hair fall in strands from the nest she had gathered on her head. I sometimes wondered whether my mother might need my help, in some way. Some guidance.

"Nejla, let's both wear green," I would say before the aunts came, going to her room to find her long, flowing dress—the one that suddenly changed her. (And if ever she put on the gold necklace as well, with the tiny stones, I wouldn't even need to collect points.)

But my mother would give me that look, as if trying to determine who I was. And then, she would look her wildest for our visitors. It was as if she wanted all of us to declare that she was mad and leave her alone.

When the aunts sat in the kitchen with her, she smoked one cigarette after the other while she cooked.

"Really, Nejla," the aunts said each time, "really now, what an example for Nunu."

My mother let the ash collect at the tip of the cigarette, threatening to fall into the food. But no matter how hard she tried, I could still see the act—her faint smile beneath her stubbornness, with the cigarette hanging from her mouth as if she were a cowboy.

DURING BAYRAM HOLIDAYS, WHEN MY GRANDMOTHER CAME from Aldere and joined the aunts—her sisters—for conversations around the kitchen table, I pretended to be bored so my mother wouldn't feel left out. But I loved these spontaneous congregations that revealed a wealth of wisdom and knowledge in otherwise regular women.

In the company of women, everything had a name and would fall to its designated place in the world. When one of the neighbors' daughters stopped coming over for tea, I heard the aunts say that she was only going through her young girl's times. The girl's mother told them that her daughter sat hugging the pillow to make herself disappear, and all the others laughed. I was struck by the accuracy of the description and was surprised at the way the women received the news, as if it were a predictable time in every girl's life.

Unlike my mother who ignored certain changes until the time I reached middle school, no topic was embarrassing in the company of women. Asuman and Saniye would call attention to my frequent disappearances to the toilet, or my newly silken legs.

The first time I revealed my smooth legs in shorts, which my mother had observed without a word, Asuman said nonchalantly that she hoped they were waxed, because I would have no way out once I started shaving.

Women had invisible pantries of wisdom for losing weight, for varicose veins, for reducing cellulite. They were all literate in measurements for cooking—the size of matchboxes, the width of palms. Their recipes called for the thickness of orange peel, the consistency of earlobes, the thinness of sheets. I loved their powers and their control over the world.

One time, when my mother and I were leaving the aunts, a neighbor woman urged us to stay a bit longer, so we could at least eat something. Asuman told her on our behalf that my mother was impatient like that.

"She gets antsy if she stays in one place," she said. I was pleased that the ways of my mother should have such a simple and undramatic description.

In the company of women, tragedy was soothed, woven into life and routine. It was brought down to earth from its cloud of confusion. Groups of women had a way of kneading the world, firmly and skillfully, the way my grandmother kneaded her dough. She worked the sticky mixture calmly, with the certainty that the dough would eventually yield, just as groups of women could clear up spilled foods and piles of dishes within a matter of minutes, and always with the same repose.

At funerals and at sickbeds, the women busied themselves with cooking and serving tea. They gave out tasks, counted the heads of guests, matched them to the number of plates. They served soup and funeral *helva*, measuring in equal ladles, as if their careful distribution would smooth out the sorrow.

In the company of women, remembering simply meant listing. During their kitchen conversations, my grandmother and her sisters would suddenly recall a woman called Sıdıka, who had lived downstairs, and they would begin listing all the neighbors who had lived in their building. They remembered all the names for the Kanlıca grocery and its different owners. There was one Ersen Efendi with a stutter, and the task of buying vegetables from him without laughing was among the prized items on their memory list.

They listed their favorite porcelain, crystal, silver, and cloths. They remembered that the organza silk from Cyprus had supplied not just Saniye's high-waisted skirt, but my grandmother's shirt and matching purse as well. They listed the ingredients for desserts, the dishes that filled their mother's tables. They listed the games they played and their variations: marbles could be played with three pieces or five; blindman's buff with two blindfolds was called "You or Me." They listed all the films with Türkan Şoray and with Doris Day, the family ties of the characters from the series *Roots*, the rise and fall of fortunes in *Dynasty*.

"What was that song . . . ?" one of them said, and they started singing the other songs of that region. My grandmother made sure that no one jumped ahead, from Aegean songs to Anatolian; from their mother's daily repertoire to the special songs she sang when she was melancholy. There were also the ones their father sang at the dinner table, when they sat silently with their heads down. And in remembering those songs, they sang with their heads down, as if the song could not be separated from its memory.

"What was that saying . . . ?" they would say. "Remember the restaurant . . . ?" The memories contained nothing more than their items.

To be sure, there were hierarchies, and the relationships of the congregation's individual members were dictated by their ranks. Asuman had never been married, so she could not understand certain things. Saniye, similarly, had not experienced motherhood. But she, unlike my grandmother, had been in love with her husband, and her love grew with each passing year into mythical proportions, giving her superiority over her sisters. Without her late husband to correct the memory, Saniye told an everintensifying love story with a taste of real happiness her sisters could not imagine. But during the congregation, these ranks were set aside and the women were united in their ordered and arranged wisdom, just like the perfectly starched and folded linen in their closets.

Even great misfortunes were itemized. Asuman's list began with the three-wheel bicycle she was never allowed to ride and continued through the ensuing injustices she suffered as a younger sibling. Saniye listed all the times her husband's ghost appeared to her, starting with the day of his burial, when he was putting on his cuff links in the bedroom. Each subsequent visit was remembered by the ghost's careful attention to clothing, folding his handkerchiefs, polishing his shoes, or buttoning the same vest he wore on the day of his death in Aldere.

My grandmother had also untangled the torments of her mother-in-law to a list of the hand-me-downs she was forced to wear. The shelves of her grievances were stacked with the Marseille silk bought for her sister-in-law and the dresses she had to wear with the zipper open when she was pregnant with my mother.

Sometimes, cheered on by her sisters—for the congregation of women produced this ebullience—my grandmother told the story of the weeks leading to my parents' wedding. It was my favorite list, and it was only told in my mother's absence. My grandmother recounted the trips to the bazaar, the dinners and lunches, the relatives that came from as far away as Antalya.

Asuman remembered the engagement dinner, listing the dishes, as if they were proof of real happiness. Saniye said that the songs that night were unforgettable, naming the solos and the duets, remembering, finally, the French song my parents sang together. At the end of the song, my father had brought out the gold necklace with the tiny stones—the same one that pulled my mother from shadows to light during my childhood—and put it around my mother's neck himself.

When the world was listed item by item, one-time events became routines, a story of the way things had always been. This, too, was the pleasure of the inventory, the shortest memories drawn out to stand in for the regularity of everyday lives.

28.

(What Luke didn't say, whenever he pointed out that every-one had a story to tell, was that it is a privilege to have a story, to know your own narrative as surely as you know your name.)

29.

It must have been in February when I met M. for the second time, because he wrote that we should go on a walk to see the Judas trees before they flowered. Then, we could enjoy the early blooms even more, later. It was just like him, this peculiar suggestion. His appreciation of unblossomed beauty.

We decided to meet in the afternoon, at the Luxembourg metro exit. I record it here as a moment of change in our correspondence: the practicality, the switch to clocks and meeting spots.

M. was waiting across the street from the metro. When he saw me, he took out his hand from his coat pocket and held it up for a moment. When I crossed the street, he leaned forward slightly, and said, "Hello again."

He appeared like a stranger, older and more stunted than the voice I had grown used to in those weeks—the one who wrote with gentle authority.

We walked into the gardens, following the outer path along the gates. I had forgotten that M. was very tall, despite his stoop. He dug his hands heavily into his pockets, as if to lower himself.

We walked in silence for a while, he on the right and I on the left. I asked him how he had been since I last saw him, realizing immediately how strange it was to ask this. We'd been writing to each other up until our meeting. Just the evening before, M. had told me about his readings on the Bronze Age. It was a period that fascinated him and he talked about it not as a faraway past, but as if it were still unraveling.

He looked at me without responding, then he stepped in front of me abruptly, moving to my left side.

"Better this way," he said. I thought that he might hear better with his right ear, but I did not ask. Several times during those weeks of our correspondence, M. had commented on his age. He said that he was perhaps too old to remember correctly when I questioned some detail about Istanbul (he remembered there were blue mosaics at the Kadıköy ferry port; I asked if he wasn't thinking of the Beşiktaş port instead), or he said in response to a story I recounted that, at my age, he certainly did not see the world with such precision. I accepted his comments in silence, feeling benevolent, with the illusory superiority endowed by my youth.

Later, I learned that there was nothing wrong with M.'s hearing but that he simply felt more comfortable walking on the left.

So let me add this detail as well, to the blurry portrait of my friend, tall and stooped, with a scar on his forehead, walking at my left side.

We walked on in almost complete silence. There were many things I wanted to tell him, but I didn't know how to start a conversation with this person walking by my side. It was as if between our arms stood an invisible wall and I had to climb over it to be able to talk to the other M. I was waiting for a sign from him, hoping he would continue one of our written conversations of the previous weeks. Anything that might consolidate the distance between the two M.'s. But M.—the one walking by my side—did not make any effort to overcome this wall. I wonder whether he felt a similar estrangement, or if he was simply observing my different states.

When I try to remember him, I sometimes have this same feeling of exhaustion, of someone behind a wall whose entirety is hidden from me, but appears in patches. It tires me to try to bring these patches together and after a while I release them from my mind's weakening grip and let them float back to their separate corners: the tall man, the writer, the hesitant hand appearing from the pocket, the wandering, distant stare.

WHEN WE HAD WALKED THE ENTIRE COURSE OF THE GARDEN gates, arriving back at the metro stop, M. suddenly broke the silence, pointing at the Judas tree ahead of us with its barren branches.

"Your mother's trees," he said.

I was a bit surprised by this reference, as if a stranger had eavesdropped on a private conversation.

"Oh, right," I said.

"I was struck by your description," M. continued, "and by all your memories of your mother. And I was very touched that you shared them with me.

"What a special bond," he said. "The two of you had your own world. I've never known a relationship like yours. And I'm so sad I didn't know you in Istanbul, so I could have included your city in my books."

We had reached the gate and I pointed across the street to the bistro with the red awning.

"Time for lunch," I said, and M. laughed with delight.

30.

All this, as I said, is in the past. These days it seems naïve, if not misguided, to retreat from the real city. And it's hard to talk about Istanbul without mentioning the fate that has befallen it.

Those who continue to talk of Istanbul's beauty are certainly far away from it. Inside the city, first and foremost, there is that constant hum. And the crowds. So much loneliness in the midst of so many people.

Istanbul presses down on us, heavier each day. It's becoming harder to ignore it, even if I sometimes feel that I'm as much a stranger here as I was in Paris.

But I know that the city is saying something and that its message is growing louder. I don't doubt that its meaning will soon become clear, whether I listen to it or not.

It's a futile exercise, this inventory I'm making of a vanished friendship. It's a way to pass the short time before something else takes over.

31.

After M. and I left the gardens, we had lunch at Au Petit Suisse across the street. It's the bistro with the narrow terrace, some steps away from the more popular café, all in lime green, on one corner of the Place Edmond-Rostand.

I can still picture it perfectly, and I feel a pang to think that life can be continuing there as always, sunlight filtering in streams in the early afternoon, the regulars taking their tables without giving any notice, tourists lingering outside, reading the cluttered menu.

M. and I took the back table. After this first lunch, we went there several times and always sat in the same corner. We called this place "our bistro." The one on Saint-Michel, where we had a drink on our first walk, was "the night café." We called the Luxembourg metro exit "the spot."

"Let's meet tomorrow, at the spot," we would say, or, "How about a drink at the night café?"

Let me put down a few more things, in case I forget to mention them later. There was "Sir Winston," the old waiter at our bistro, who brought us two pieces of chocolate each with our coffees. "The philosopher" was the sulky waiter who served the tables outside. We referred to anyone with spiritual inclinations as "crystal hunters." Those who approached life with the insincere compassion of self-help books we called "dictators." I don't remember which one of us came up with this title or why—I don't think I would have told M. about Luke. But I told him that my mother had always been suspicious of such "dictators" as well.

"I wish I could have known this brilliant woman," M. said.

I've already mentioned that "The Invention of Midnight" was one of our codes, and there were others like it, such as "Apollodorus," which was shorthand for forgotten writers, but also for the rapid passing of time. The name came from a few lines I read in Akif amca's journal by a Greek poet, Apollodorus, from whose work only two lines of poetry survived. (Who at such a time / has come to the edge of the doorway?) In the journal, Akif amca had written that these lines were like "pillars excavated in the desert."

"The Apollodoruses of the world," we might have said, or "in the tyrannical reign of Apollodorus," by which we would have meant that life was too short.

I'm aware that our lexicon sounds bizarre when listed like

this, and that it is slowly losing its meaning. I cannot say what would be lost with its disappearance, but these are some of the facts of our friendship.

DURING OUR FIRST LUNCH AT THE BISTRO, I SAT FACING THE gardens, upon M.'s suggestion. He suggested it without ceremony, pointing at the chair.

"You sit here," he said.

He examined the menu the moment we sat down, looking up and down the pages quickly, then set it aside. He listed the dishes we should share, more as a statement of fact than to ask for confirmation. We had endive with scallops, terrine, marinated sardines, and also beet salad with goat cheese, upon Sir Winston's recommendation.

I remember that M. spoke French clumsily, making many mistakes, but without apology. Waiters never reverted to English with him, as they sometimes did with me, even though my French was probably better, certainly more correct, from my studies at university. But especially in M.'s presence, I spoke slowly, carefully picking every word.

When our food arrived ("Bring everything at once," M. told Sir Winston, "we like eating in the Mediterranean style"), M. ate with appetite and without fussing. He dipped his bread in mustard and swept the contents of his plate—cheese, salad, fish, meat—on top of it. His manner when he ate was different from the thoughtful, quiet way he wrote, and also from his reserve in person. I often had the feeling that if I focused hard enough, I would be able to see him clearly. And I should say that with some effort, I would have seen myself clearly.

During my friendship with M., I began to remember something about myself I had been looking away from. A wordless, soundless knowledge. I realized that I could look at it directly and it would have a surprising shape, neither ugly nor shameful.

But this was only a glimpse. I told myself I would allow it to emerge, when the time was right. But that is no different from keeping it at bay.

32.

Some years after my father's death, when I was nine or ten, I was given a book about fairies by my mother's Welsh friend, Robert, a soft-spoken photographer who came to Istanbul every year. I wanted to become friends with Robert, quickly and irreversibly. I wanted to list him among members of my family.

This book was my prized possession and it contained photographs of flower fairies in English gardens. My delight with the book, apart from the fact that Robert had given it to me, was simple: the photographs were undeniable proof of an existence that otherwise escaped our limited gaze. I examined them again and again, the tiny creatures whose frail bodies of half-light were not unlike the flower petals around which they hovered. My favorite photograph, which I had looked at so many times that the book's spine obediently opened itself to that page, was a black-and-white one of a fairy child around my age wearing a white skirt. At the moment the picture was taken, she had ducked her head behind the speckled bell of a foxglove. The photo made it clear to me why I had never seen these shy and darting creatures myself. In the background, the tenants of the estate—a couple in hats, tall and thin—were walking down the garden path without the slightest awareness of the magic unraveling in the distance.

Robert brought my mother presents as well—a dark purple scarf, books, a fountain pen. One time, he gave her a blue bowl painted with birds, and I thought this was the most beautiful thing I had ever seen. But it didn't seem to me that my mother prized these gifts as I did my book of fairies. She often packed them and brought them to my grandmother in Aldere.

I had once climbed on Robert's lap with my fairy book when he asked me to show him my favorite pictures. My mother came into the room briefly, then left, and we heard her loudly stacking dishes in the kitchen. I wanted to tell Robert that my mother was not always like this, that he kept missing her moments of light and color just like one would miss the mischievous fairies in the gardens. Robert, as far as I knew, had only once seen her in the green dress, and never with the necklace.

"Uncle Robert," I called him—Robert amca—and I made a point of saying it often, enjoying the bond of familiarity I could create with a single word.

"When is Robert amca coming?"

"Isn't Robert amca kind?"

"Nejla, tell this story to Robert amca as well!"

I must have been in middle school when my mother said there was no need to call him that.

"He's not your uncle," she said.

I remember that my mother stacked things away like this, as she did Robert's presents, her friends, the concerns of her aunts. She put them away and wrote them off, and she ignored that she could hurt others in this way.

But what I remember now is something else: There was a time when I understood her. I knew that she felt she had no other choice.

33.

The symmetrical letter with which I represent M., offering a tip of the hat to the neat symmetries of fiction, is an invention. For each of his readers, his name will recall a different person. Of course, it wouldn't be too difficult to solve the puzzle of M.'s identity, but I still prefer this single letter, while I list some aspects of our friendship, brief though it may be, separate from whatever his name conjures for others.

For a long time, I thought of writers as people with a sort of immunity, with the power to shape events in whichever way they wanted. The title of writer was mysterious, even mythical; it was separate from the world.

And from time to time, I thought of M. in this way as well. Even when he wrote to me, I felt that he was in two places at once, forming daily events into another story, and that whatever path our friendship took, it would inevitably become what M. wanted it to be.

ONE TIME, WHEN M. ADDRESSED ME IN AN E-MAIL, "SILENT ONE with her head down," I wondered immediately whether he was trying out these very words for a character. Another time when we were walking across the Pont de la Tournelle and saw the cathedral in its rising, spreading grandeur, we both paused, and even though I wished for the moment to be shared, I thought that M. was in another place, where he was master, where he alone felt the full weight of the world. But to distinguish myself from all the other readers who surely looked up to him, I did not tell him I had read his novels.

And there were things I never asked, no matter our peculiar conversations. I would have liked to know what he ate for breakfast; his favorite film or joke; what he was like as a child. But I thought that these were not fitting questions to ask a writer.

Sometimes during a long walk, when I felt that we saw the city through the same eyes, when our conversation flowed effortlessly and would continue to do so for hours to come, M. would look at his watch and say, "Sadly, it's time for me to go."

This statement never ceased to startle me.

It was moments like these that made me think that our friendship meant different things to me and M. At least, it was in those moments that I realized M. had other worlds in which he was equally at ease, and to which he was eager to return.

34.

My first year at university, I shared a room with a curly-haired girl called Molly. She was from Manchester and she did everything with ease. The best way I can describe it is that she was thoroughly acquainted with herself; fully and without flinching, and she did not resist any part of this self-knowledge.

In the evenings, while I sat at my desk revising or writing, she lay in bed and moved her legs in the air as if she were cycling.

Some mornings she said, "I can't be bothered to go to class, Nunu, so listen extra hard."

She commented on the way I dressed, the way I talked, the way I had arranged my side of the room with paper garlands and black-and-white photographs. Her comments sounded as if she knew me thoroughly, too, just as she knew herself, and had seen nothing disturbing. It surprised me to see myself through her eyes.

"You're so inventive," she said. "How're you so inventive?"

I told Molly that my mother was this way, even though I didn't say that her originality was of a different kind.

In answering Molly's questions, I created a parallel life that seemed like something from a book or a film. I told her that I had never really known my father. He'd died when I was little, I said, and I could barely remember him.

I told Molly that my mother had always treated me as an adult and that I had grown up doing things that would have been unusual for other children. (Later, to Luke, I told another story altogether.)

"How exotic," Molly said.

When she talked to her parents on the phone she told them about all the things she had done that week. She mentioned if she'd eaten something delicious and she complained about her assignments.

"I'm sorry to tell you that your daughter's an idiot," she said.

I would be at my desk, studying.

"Meanwhile, my brilliant roommate can write an essay with her eyes closed."

I turned around and waved my hand as a message for her parents.

"She says hi," Molly said. "She also says, 'I'm so gloomy and mysterious and I'm going to stop reading and go out with Molly tonight.'"

On the first school holiday, her parents invited me to visit them in Manchester.

"They want to meet my Turkish friend," Molly said. "Please, please come and make me happy."

I slept in Molly's bed and Molly slept on a mattress on the floor. At night, she told me about all the things she wanted to do, not discriminating between her future and her plans for the following day. I remember that she wanted to go to the Galápagos Islands, and she said "Galápagos" as if she alone knew its meaning.

Molly's father drove us around the city and took us to the docks where Molly asked him in a playful, whiny voice for honey-roasted almonds. We each got a cone and Molly walked between me and her father, taking both our arms.

On the last day of our visit I offered to make dinner. Molly's mother said they all loved Turkish food. I remember the feeling it gave me to hear their opinions in plural, that familiar "we," all of them converging around the things they loved.

I called the aunts to ask for a recipe. It was something simple—white bean stew with rice—and I explained to my hosts that this was "a family dinner," the type of thing we would have on a weekday. I was aware of the image they might have, of a loud and crowded Mediterranean family gathered around a steaming pot. The type of family where sorrow is less sorrowful because it mingles with merriness and plentitude, turns into comedy. It was with such a picture of my imaginary family that I told my hosts that my great-aunts would faint if they saw this dinner I had made, which was nothing more than peasant fare.

"Your family is just the best," Molly said.

"What a treat," Molly's mother said when we sat down.

She told me I was always welcome in their home. She repeated that it was a treat to have me there.

Molly said, "Why couldn't you guys raise me a bit more like Nunu? See how well she turned out?"

I repeated Molly's sentences in my head, making jokes, narrating events, saying things in her carefree way. I imagined talking this way to my mother when I returned for the summer holiday. I had never been cheerful around her or delighted her the way Molly did her parents. I remember thinking—I had been away from Istanbul for several months then, and it is easy to forget the texture of a relationship—that I would go back and take charge, with these new cheerful ways.

From the time we were roommates until my mother's death, Molly wanted to visit me in Istanbul. I always said we should plan this trip and that it would be fun. But each time I went back, I found an excuse to delay her trip. Perhaps I was afraid that Molly would see something else when she finally met my mother; that I would be found out.

35.

On the days leading up to our walks, M. did not write to me, except for an e mail to confirm our meeting time and place; this was a different language than the one we otherwise used. Perhaps he wanted to keep our two conversations separate or he was simply waiting to talk to me in person and would use the saved time for his own work. He never hinted that he did not have time to write to me, nor that he was much busier than I was. But this was all evident from the specific days and hours he suggested for our walks (never on Tuesdays or Thursdays, always in the late afternoon).

And perhaps I preferred our written friendship to our walks, because of its abundance of conversation and its directness. "Listen to this—"

But even though I preferred writing to him, I glowed when I walked with M.

So much of the texture of a relationship disappears when shaped into stories—all the feeling residing beneath the spoken words. (When we first moved from Moda to the new apartment, I would climb up to my mother's bed in the afternoons when she lay looking at the ceiling. After a while, I would lift my hand and put it on her shoulder. My mother didn't move, and she didn't say anything. I extended my arm across her chest, until I reached her opposite shoulder. I tried not to hold too tight, not to tire her. My mother kept still but I could almost hear her silent acknowledgment.

But sometimes, sometimes, she moved her leg to my side, all the while looking at the ceiling, her knee barely grazing mine.)

This period when I was friends with M. was not just made up of our words. There was a particularity to it, something that will, with time, disappear, unless I record, as truthfully as I can, what I remember.

THERE WAS A SINGLE MIRROR IN MY STUDIO, A SMALL, CRACKED one above the sink, and I would stand in front of it for a long time before leaving the house to meet M. Since arriving in Paris, my hair, which had been short and boyish all my life, had grown to the sides of my chin, swallowing my face. I looked pale, I thought, and my eyes protruded with a relentless darkness. Some find this an attractive quality about me. Luke called it enigmatic. And while I did not object, I felt foreign to the compliment, if that's what it was. I thought that it was a way of saying something else. But whenever I met M. for a walk, I felt my features softening to regular proportions, becoming acceptable, even pleasant.

And something else: the more beautiful I felt, the older M. became. I felt radiant, even while I cast my eyes down on the ground. And as I glowed, M. aged. The word that comes to me now to describe him is *stammering*. When we met at our spot, M. would have a look of panic on his face and I thought that he might stumble as he took out his hand from his pocket and lifted it to greet me. And then we started walking and I looked down at the ground, feeling shy and nervous next to this man who appeared like a stranger each time, and feeling beautiful nevertheless.

But something usually happened to smooth out his hesitation. For example, M. might tell me a fact about Istanbul I had never known. Or he would draw out a particular detail from an anecdote I wrote to him and say that I should include it in my novel. Or he would simply look at his watch and say that he had to get going. Whatever it was, I would suddenly see M. with his full name, the name of the author, and he would no longer be the stammering man next to whom I walked with glowing confidence.

36.

When I was in middle school, the aunts began hosting a weekly Sufi meeting held in Saniye's apartment, where neighbors gathered to listen to an elderly woman they called Sultan, as if calling her by any other, worldlier name would be a slight to her wisdom. It would have been easier for me to glimpse Sultan's wisdom had she worn a veil, carried rosary beads, or even acted in the ways of the spiritually endowed, closing her eyes or rocking in her chair. Instead, she wore plain shirts and trousers and draped a cotton cloth loosely around her head before the gatherings, devoid of ritual. But she had a shock of silver hair and bright green eyes and it was said that she had received the blessing of the Baghdadi Sheikh Abdülkadir Geylani in a dream.

I once asked the aunts exactly what had happened in Sultan's dream and Asuman said, without providing me with any more clarity, that Geylani had given Sultan his hand, touching not just her heart but her soul. Such dreams, Asuman told me, were the bridge between two separate worlds and aligned them on a single path, so that from then on, the soul would walk in both places at once.

"Our Sultan is very special," Saniye added. "She can explain things to you that your mother can't talk about."

But the Sufi meetings were not very different from the tea parties my grandmother used to host for the wives of Aldere. The neighborhood women competed to feed Sultan with pound cakes, cookies, stuffed grape leaves, and cheese pastries. While they waited for her arrival, they swapped recipes, careful not to give away the key ingredients of Sultan's favorite dishes.

The gatherings were called "conversations" and I sensed that this title, like Sultan's dream, bridged two separate worlds, and referred to a conversation with invisible beings.

The conversations began with the telling of dreams. Regular participants knew how to interpret them in the Sufi manner. Even I knew that dreaming of physical touch meant the transfer of knowledge, or that water signified purity. Some participants inserted telltale symbols of wisdom into their dreams—peacocks, doves, roses—in order to gain Sultan's favor. Others were so keen to read the dreams as a set of clues that could unlock the doors to enlightenment that they attributed spiritual significance to the most mundane objects. Second-rate newspapers, which I read with interest whenever we visited the aunts, were full of such lists, supplying religious interpretations for cars, textiles, and animals, as well as common household goods, such as sieves, tablecloths, or toothpaste. Some of these objects had obvious meanings—cars signified journeys, of course—but others were more ambiguous, like toothpaste, which meant somehow that the dreamer would not find support from their closest of kin.

But Sultan would shake her head at these precise interpretations and remind her group that dreams were not meant as entertainment. She said that we must listen to them with our innermost heart, which knew no lies.

When she said this, I had the uneasy feeling that something was eluding me, something I would hear if only I could be honest with myself. If I were brave.

MY MOTHER DID NOT STAY IN THE ROOM FOR TOO LONG DURING the meetings. She would go to the kitchen to make tea, or sit at the window, smoking and watching the plaza. When she left the room, I felt guilty for listening with interest and followed her to the kitchen shortly afterwards.

"What happened?" she asked. "I thought you were enjoying yourself."

I shrugged, pretending to be bored.

We often left before the meetings ended, waving goodbye to the aunts from the door. To my embarrassment, Sultan would pause the conversation and say that she hoped to see us more often. My mother thanked her and said something appropriate, like, "God willing," surprising me with her etiquette.

After we left the building and were walking across the plaza, she said, "That was enough nonsense to last us a year."

But we would be back at the gathering the following week, and I would sit at the front and then my mother would leave and go to the kitchen after some time.

Perhaps she wanted me to be surrounded by all those cheerful women, dissecting the invisible world and putting it back together without a care.

37.

But that's not all. There were things my mother cherished, without excuse. She listed the actors and titles of Western movies she watched with Akif amca on Sundays. *The Lonesome Trail, The Far Country, Many Rivers to Cross*. She listed these names in the same, absent way that she smoked cigarettes with her distant stare, as if she were treading the frontiers of those faraway lands.

From these titles, I glimpsed a bright and vast world, with borders neatly separating the good from the evil. The movies' solitary heroes—in *Stranger on Horseback, Buchanan Rides Alone*— had nothing but their inner strength to overcome their tasks.

My mother remembered Akif amca's favorite film and actor (*Man of the West* and Gary Cooper), as well as the scenes he loved most, when the heroes emerged, triumphant, from their troubles. Once or twice, when they left the cinema, my mother had objected to the impossibility of the plots, and the films' glorious endings. But Akif amca told her, with certainty, that life progressed in such surprising leaps and that what she witnessed in these films was indeed the way of the world.

My mother repeated his words to me whenever the two of us watched a Western, on weekend afternoons when we didn't leave the apartment.

"That's the way of the world, Nunu. That's what Akif amca said."

Certainly, she could not have believed this, but I think she wanted me to hear these words as well, in case I made better use of them.

38.

found echoes of my conversations with M. all around me, in the books I read, the conversations I overheard at the Café du Coin, the sights on my own walks, as if the world had tightened into a web of signs and symbols. It wasn't unlike being in love. But at the time I wouldn't have said that exactly. Not in that way.

The coincidences were mostly amusing but pointless, like the time M. wrote to me about his fondness for pigeons. He said that these birds, with their bleak urban colors, their crippled claws, and their unendangered abundance, living their lives right in our midst, had always filled him with melancholy. That afternoon, when I was walking to Les Halles past the fishmongers on rue Montorgueil, I noticed all the pigeons wandering around on the wet pavement beneath the stalls. I thought that M.'s compassion towards such unremarkable creatures was typical of the way he saw the world, just like our first meeting to look at the dry

Judas trees in the Luxembourg Gardens. I'd thought at the time that it was probably just an excuse to go on a walk, but I realized later that M. had been sincere. He felt endearment for the pathetic, and I worried that I was one among them. Just after I turned off rue Montorgueil, I passed the window display of a natural history bookshop—usually filled with books on seashells, gems, palm trees—and saw that it was covered entirely with prints of pigeons.

Other coincidences were stranger, like the time I told M. that my mother loved Westerns because they reminded her of Akif amca. I said that the landscape of my mother's childhood in Aldere was superimposed on another, vaster landscape she had never seen. I did not quite believe my own description but I liked the neat articulation. I also said that even though I did not particularly enjoy these movies, I had watched many of them with my mother, and listed the titles, actors, and quotes, much to M.'s surprise.

"You should write this story down," M. said.

"Which one?"

"The young girl in a Thracian village, learning about life from cowboys."

Some minutes later, we walked past a cinema with a poster of a Western movie hanging at its entrance. As we were laughing at the coincidence, we noticed that the last names of the two lead actors combined made up M.'s own name.

"I guess it means I have to write the story myself," M. said.

The coincidences always amazed me even if I knew that they

were neither miracles nor revelations but the result of looking at the world deliberately and searching for connections.

M. treated these moments as nothing more than our harmony with our surroundings. He told me one time that being in tune to the invisible threads that connected us through time and space was a state he usually achieved only in the depths of writing.

"You sound like a crystal hunter," I said.

"I've been meaning to confess to you . . . ," M. said.

We were sitting on a bench at the Place Dauphine. We had not eaten all day, and it was already too late to go to our bistro. M. was invited to an event that evening, which, he said, was a gathering of all the old fools in Paris.

He loved to say this—"old fool"—and he said it often, about himself and about others, but I don't know what he thought made everyone so foolish.

"There are so many old fools," he said. "They continue doing their foolish old things, growing blinder by the day."

But it now occurs to me that he actually said these things not as self-deprecation but out of compassion, to undermine his activities and acquaintances, when he must have known that I had no one in the city but him.

I took out an apple from my bag and bit into it, wiping the juice that trickled down my chin with my hand. I noticed that M. was watching me and smiling.

The evening had set all at once and M. put his hands deep into his pockets as he often did when he was getting ready to leave.

Then he got up, took one hand out of his pocket, and instead of waving like he usually did, extended it towards me as if he were handing me something that he held between his thumb and index finger.

"I'll cross the city unspooling our invisible thread," he said. "Hold tight to the other end."

I have since wondered what invisible connection he made as he walked away, leaving me to eat my apple.

39.

During university, I took a class on Sufism taught by an English professor who had spent some time with a Sufi group in Bulgaria. I took several classes like this, on topics I was familiar with—history of the Ottoman Empire, Middle Eastern politics. At first, I registered for them because I thought they would get me an easy grade, and provide relief from more difficult subjects, which they did. But I soon realized that whatever I said in these classes was given extra attention, as if I were a guest lecturer. My classmates looked to me during difficult discussions, professors asked me for anecdotes. In the end, I actually studied hardest for these classes, to keep up the image that I was an expert. And with this unexpected attention, I began to feel something like indignation, or smugness; as if I were claiming what had been my right all along.

On the first day of the Sufism class, when we were introducing ourselves, I announced that I belonged to the Sufi order of Ab-dülkadir Geylani in Istanbul. I was astonished at the ease with which I could say this, aware of my exaggeration and how exotic it sounded.

Whenever I saw the professor around campus, he smiled brightly and came over to talk to me. He even invited me to dinner at his house one Christmas holiday when I didn't go back to Istanbul. He presented me to his wife as the Geylani disciple.

Their house was filled with rugs and Persian miniatures. His wife showed me the blue ceramics they had collected around Turkey. I remember she had cooked something that seemed strange a tagine, perhaps, with dried fruits that I found unusual at the time. And I remember that they served tea with dinner. I think they didn't want to offend me, my Sufi upbringing, with alcohol.

At the end of my second year, the professor asked me to help him with his research and I quickly accepted, canceling my plans to visit my mother. I enjoyed being this other person, away from Istanbul, surrounded by people who found me enchanting, whom I'd learned to enchant with fictionalized versions of myself.

I told my mother on the phone that I would spend the break working. My mother didn't insist, and I told myself that she didn't mind. I used to tell Molly stories of my independent mother, how devoted she was to her work and routine.

"She's probably lost in her readings," I said, with a hazy picture in my mind of an eccentric woman buried in books.

"God, you're lucky," Molly said. "My parents would call the police or something if they didn't hear from me for two days."

In my absence, my mother had painted the walls of my room and put up new bookshelves. She asked me on the phone what color wood I preferred; whether I would like a new desk.

When I went to Istanbul the following vacation, I spent most of my time out of the apartment. I met up with my high school friends, Selin, Ezgi, Defne, who were also back for vacation from abroad. We were eager to compare our lives, discuss our new ideas and interests. We went on explorations of the old town, seeing it for the first time with the same interest shown us at our universities abroad. We went to the Grand Bazaar to buy touristic knick-knacks to take back—evil-eye beads, ceramic bowls, backgammon boards. We were enthralled by the possibilities of our new identities, the way we could shape them any way we wanted to.

On that trip, I visited the aunts and even went to Sultan's gatherings, though my mother and I had stopped attending them when I was in high school. I stayed behind to ask Sultan questions about the history of the order and the proper conduct of a disciple, hoping to return to university with new information. Sultan was very old then, and did not remember many things. She spoke slowly, repeating herself throughout a conversation, talking in circles. Her answers were vague. She said that the specifics did not so much matter as a willingness to set out on the path. But she was more eager to talk about her youth in Kanlıca, her trips to Europe, her parents' home on the Black Sea coast.

I would sometimes spend the night at the aunts' and they were delighted.

"Nunu's staying over because she needs to be fed!" they told my mother on the phone. "Her aunts are preparing a feast for this poor lamb."

When I came home, I would go directly to my room. I only wandered around the apartment if my mother was in her bedroom. I left early in the mornings, calling out from the doorway that I was going out, with barely enough time for my mother to come to the hallway before I closed the door.

"Would you like to have fish in Yeniköy?" she asked in a hurry. "Shall we have a lazy breakfast tomorrow?"

I told her I would be out with my friends. Sometimes I only shrugged.

I had not planned to act like this, but once I gave in to it, I felt that the silence had no end. This was different from the silence of my childhood. It kept growing—this meanness inside me I had never known.

40.

We would meet at our spot—the exit of the Luxembourg metro—and M. would ask if I had a destination in mind. I usually said no, and we started walking in whatever direction we happened to be facing. M. never minded the rain or the cold and always wore the same dark green jacket, which seemed to adapt to every weather. We often walked into the gardens, tracing the periphery, weaving in and out of the paths, the beehives by Vavin, the Senate walls, the fountain, the circle of marble queens, whose cryptic and subtle facial expressions we discussed on several occasions. It was difficult to say whether they were content or suffering. ("Sometimes," M. wrote to me, "I can barely tell apart my sorrow from my joy when I'm writing." Immediately, I recognized the statement as a truth.)

If I arrived early, I went into the gardens knowing I would find M. there, sitting on a chair by the side of the fountain. He didn't see me. He would be bent over his notebook and I imagined that he was writing to me, even though we only wrote to each other by e-mail.

The sight of him from a distance was familiar. His green jacket, his long, crossed legs and thoughtful frown. He looked like an old man and also like a young boy, and watching him from a distance, I felt that I could focus on all of him at once. After some time, I turned back and walked to our spot by the metro to wait, and after a while he appeared across the street, taking his hand out of his pocket to greet me.

Some days we walked down rue de Seine or rue Bonaparte to the river. We passed by the lively cafés, art galleries, map shops, and patisseries with fantastical displays, all of which, we agreed, were more beautiful from a distance, without pausing to look for too long. As such they retained the unspoiled sense of a neighborhood full of possibilities. Before we emerged from the sheltered world of Saint-Germain, M. pointed out the Alpine bookshop, which he admired for the specificity of its books. He admitted that he'd never actually been inside this shop, whose subject matter did not particularly interest him, but said that he was happy it was there. In his love for these peculiar places, he was like an anthropologist, or an accountant. I couldn't quite tell which, because I was never certain what lay beneath M.'s fascinations. Sometimes I imagined that they were a sign of sorrow, a wish to care for and preserve things on the brink of disappearance. Other times, I thought that they were nothing more than a tedious desire to accumulate.

"Here it is," M. said, every time we passed the bookshop. "I'm so happy someone thought of such a place."

He said it in the same way each time, as if he were experienc-ing the joy afresh. Then, one afternoon, he said, "You never tell me I've told you this before. You're kind to humor this old fool."

"I know you like the shop," I said.

I also knew that things don't loosen their grip so easily, with a single utterance.

When we reached the river, we took the stairs down to the water, following the line of poplars all the way to the winged horses of the Pont Alexandre III, then back, up past where we had descended the stairs. We often went to the flower market on Île de la Cité and walked its two short stretches multiple times, for the pleasure of being among the potted palms, camellias, and ol-ives. When we walked off the island, we went in the direction of Châtelet so that we could walk past the blue-and-gold clock stud-ded with stars on the Conciergerie, and one of us would invariably say something, then, about "The Invention of Midnight."

M. did not mind the repetition of these walks, the way a child will not tire of listening to a favorite story. It amazed me that we always walked the most beautiful parts of the city, what might even be called the city's clichés. If I were guiding us on our walks, I might have saved them for special occasions, as one saves wed-ding china and silk dresses. But M. was not sparing with beauty; he lived it fully and constantly, shared it generously.

We went into museums like veering off into alleyways. These visits were never planned and we walked through the exhibits as if they were city streets, without really stopping, pausing only if something caught our attention. M. was more attentive in small, municipal museums than at the grand ones full of visitors. He mostly looked around him quickly, at times making a small sound of recognition or surprise.

"That's something," he said from time to time. Then, without waiting for me to respond, he continued walking, picking up our conversation where we had left it.

Now, it surprises me even more that M. and I could surround ourselves with beauty and not pay particular attention to it. I feel that we were always breaking the rules, defying the proper way to do something. Perhaps I only say this because life here in Istanbul now is so deprived of these indulgences.

41.

Even when we don't have the heart to read the papers, are too worried to consider all the possibilities, and have lost count of all that's vanished, we continue to talk about Taksim Square. It is the cliché of the changing times. Or perhaps its symbol.

The square is unrecognizable now, this much is true. There are the old black-and-white photographs of the tram running down İstiklal in winter, blurred by snow, the chestnut sellers looking on. These pictures resurface time and again in outraged newspapers, as if to press on our wound.

Some are still protesting to salvage scraps. But it's easier to give it up, without struggle. To say, "Alright, you have this as well, take it and do what you will. Take it all, change it completely." With the hope that we may be left in peace, even if it's on one tiny plot of land.

But there's no denying that it's a shock to see the square—to walk up İstiklal and emerge at Taksim expanding like a desert. And the people who gather there now, all those men without roots. They find solace in this nameless place, in its formless expanse. The orphans of the city.

42.

When I returned to Istanbul from England to take care of my mother, we pretended that I was back for vacation and that as soon as she got a bit better I would go to Paris to start the literature program. We didn't talk about the previous years, how long it had been since I'd been home.

I heard her on the phone, talking to people I'd never met. In my absence, she had made friends. Later, these friends came over with food, with flowers.

"Nunu is visiting," my mother told them on the phone. "We're finally reunited, back in our nest."

She listened to their stories with curiosity, her face showing concern and surprise. She called these friends "darling," "sweetie." I didn't know when my mother had begun to change, to become like the mothers of girls I used to know.

"You might as well make use of this time," she said to me. "Now that you're here. There are so many new places in the city."

We were still timid around each other then.

I left the house each day for a little bit, this time not to shut her out, as I'd wanted to on my previous visits, but to please her, and make her feel that she was not as sick as she really was. Besides, I could do little for her in those days, beyond keeping the household in order, and witnessing her pain.

In the mornings, I walked to the supermarket to shop for lunch or simply wander the aisles, after which I sat on a park bench to read and wait for an appropriate amount of time to pass before I returned home.

I told my mother, once or twice, that I had met up with my friends, Selin, Ezgi, and Defne, and gave her news of their lives. In reality, I no longer had any desire to see these friends, who were now settled in Istanbul with purpose and motivation after returning from their studies abroad. Two of them were engaged. They were pursuing interesting and ambitious careers. I imagined they would ask me about my news, and I would have none to give.

My mother listened eagerly whenever I talked about my friends and this, too, surprised me. During high school, she knew little about these girls and our uncomplicated friendships, formed from occasional outings around the city, and spending time at their houses after school, though I never returned the invitations.

The few times I stayed overnight, the mothers would prepare pastries and cakes, or let us order pizza. They sat with us
for a while, then left us alone when we began laughing hysteri-
cally over the smallest things. At night, they came to the bedroom to tell us they were going to sleep. We would be sitting on
the floor, listening to music or looking through magazines.

One time, Selin's mother came in and started snapping her
fingers in rhythm to the music.

"Mom, what are you doing?" Selin said. And then she said,
getting up to hug her, "She tries so hard to be cool."

WHEN I GRADUATED FROM HIGH SCHOOL, THE AUNTS URGED MY
mother to host a lunch for my friends.

"Would Nunu want any of that fuss?" my mother said, and I
responded that I wouldn't. I was uncomfortable at the thought of
my friends seeing my life at home. The aunts finally organized
the lunch themselves and invited many of my classmates. Those
days, it was fashionable to meet in Tophane to smoke hookah or
go to the Kadıköy fish market for beers and fries. My classmates
doubtless found it peculiar to gather at the home of a great-aunt,
with lace tablecloths and crystal glasses from which we drank
Fanta. But I didn't mind this. I even enjoyed my unfashionable
ordinariness.

After the lunch, I came home to tell my mother, exaggerating
the trouble the aunts had gone to, that this was one of the most
thoughtful things anyone had ever done for me.

I knew how to hurt her, too. So slyly you could hardly point to it.

"I didn't realize you would enjoy something like that," my mother said. "I thought you preferred to be alone with your friends."

43.

When I returned to Istanbul from Paris, returned here for good, that is, others were already leaving. I had been in touch with several high school friends who told me they were getting ready to move abroad, or searching for a way to do so.

"We're running away," they said. "This is no place to live."

It hurt me to hear them talking about the city like this.

The dangerous city, the tiring city, the dubious city.

Our Istanbul had become an unwanted place.

They were married, some had children; they watched their careers sway this way and that in the new political climate. They were sad that it had come to this, but they had their futures to think of. In Istanbul, they said, there was no knowing what would happen next.

And there was no denying what they said was true.

44.

ere's something else M. wrote to me. I read it many times:
"I don't think I will ever get tired of your stories."

I wrote back to say that this sounded like an easy challenge.

(To be clear, his words made me happy. But I realize now that
I had a way of sweeping away these moments casually, not giving
in to my happiness.)

"Not a challenge," M. said. "Only a sincere observation."

In my notebook, I had a list of things I wrote down to tell him
later. The shopkeeper touching her earlobe to check her gold
earring; the smell of the metro rising from grills on the pavement; the old woman at Café du Coin who ate her dessert every
afternoon with her free hand hovering protectively over the
plate, as if someone might take it away from her.

I made lists of foods, films, trees, in the way I had learned from M.'s novels, and I told them to him in the detached manner of his narrators. In this way, the people in my stories—my mother, the aunts, my child self—took on lives of their own, treading a separate path than their earthly twins. And M. was always delighted.

But I had already begun to wonder how long I could keep up this friendship with its stock of inconsequential details, and how long M. would enjoy reading my stories, which I wrote mimicking his style.

A few times, we met close to Gare du Nord and I showed him places around my neighborhood—the Saint-Quentin market, the ivy-covered plaza behind boulevard de Magenta—so that I could be in charge of our walk. I took M. to a Turkish restaurant by the Porte Saint-Denis, and ordered for us in Turkish.

"It's such a pleasure to hear you speak," M. said.

On another walk, I brought us to Café du Coin, as if we'd just happened upon it. I didn't tell M. that this was where I lived.

"I sometimes come here, because it's nice and quiet," I said.

M. remarked that I knew my way around those streets like the back of my hand.

I acted familiarly with the young waiter, and he returned the gesture, smiling at me broadly. When we were ordering, he winked and asked if "mademoiselle" would have hot chocolate with her meal.

Whenever I interacted with men my age, M. seemed different. Sadder, I suppose. Or apologetic. This made me even more fond of him.

But from time to time, he would say something that defied the unspoken rules of our friendship, and his shyness, which I liked so much, would disappear.

"My wife used to love rosé wine, just like you," he said one afternoon, when we were having lunch at our bistro. "And its alluring color certainly suited her."

Another time, after I crossed the street and we exchanged our usual greeting, he said, without a hint of the usual stammering tone, that I looked lovely.

"Of course that's no news to you," he added, "you always look lovely."

But these were rare instances.

ONE AFTERNOON, WHILE WE WERE WALKING IN FRONT OF Notre-Dame towards the flower market, M. steered us away from the plaza all the way to the other side and stopped to look at the cathedral from a distance. There was such harmony in the arrangement, he said. The craftsmen had never lost track of what they were doing. He pointed from left to right at the prophets, the kings, the apostles, the life of the Virgin.

Until then, I had only seen the front of Notre-Dame from close up and looked at the hundreds of stone faces, which seemed cluttered and without much order. I went back the following day and examined the façade carefully. The next time that we walked in front of the cathedral, I pointed out a cluster of leaves, St. Anne's sturdy hands, the marble book with blank pages, a wreath of acorns.

"The world in your step," M. wrote that evening, listing all the things I had shown him, "has more colors in its rainbow." But I didn't tell him then, nor on any other occasion, that he had taught me something new about seeing this world.

It could be tiring to create these worlds for M., for only a moment's worth of gratification. I was constantly collecting things to show him, reading about historical curiosities, memorizing lines of poetry or the unusual details of a building or bridge, and even learning feats of engineering that I would then mention offhandedly in conversation. And each time that M. expressed admiration for my wealth of knowledge and my ability to notice such minute details, I brushed his comments off as if to say that these were nothing to cause attention. This may have been my retaliation for all the times M. looked at his watch and told me he had to get going. I, too, wanted to show him that I had my places to go, that I had been places.

45.

"It's you we worry about," the aunts say. They say it every Sunday when I take them to the plaza for tea. "The city's screw has come loose."

But they worry about themselves, too.

"Just look at Kanlıca. This used to be a modern neighborhood."

They tell me they feel like foreigners in their own home and soon they'll be pushed out, no doubt. They have no idea where all these people have descended from, ignorant and angry, disregarding everyone else.

"No comfort in our own home," they say. "It's like an infestation."

It's the same conversation each time. Perhaps this is what they need to soothe their fears. Everyone, it seems, has a story to tell these days. Even if the stories are different, each is as fearful as the next.

46.

That year in Paris, part of the quays on the Right Bank leading down from Hôtel de Ville were closed to traffic. It seemed to me at the time that I would never be able to see Paris as it really was. Things were always under construction or repair. A dome, a church, a plaza, or a fountain was always hidden behind scaffolding. Recalling this now in Istanbul, it all seems so innocent, when our entire city has been dug up to build anew.

Not many people had noticed that the quays were closed to traffic, or they simply didn't change their routines, because this stretch was mostly empty. M. and I went down there to sit on a stone bench and watch the river, which had risen dramatically by late spring. Each time, M. took something out of his bag for us to eat.

"I think I have a little something," he said, as if he had just remembered, even though I knew he must have prepared it for our walk.

He would bring out thyme and cheese pastries from a Lebanese vendor in his neighborhood as well as a bottle of juice. I sometimes brought fruits or a bag of nuts and we spread the food between us on the bench.

We called these our "midnight picnics" in reference to Akif amca's poem, and without apparent reason, because we only went there during the day.

On one picnic, M. told me about an uncle who lived in America and was a heroic figure in M.'s childhood, not least because of the presents he brought on every visit. It was this same uncle who had given M. his first typewriter and encouraged him to write. A Remington model, M. remembered, whose *N* key made a whirring sound. (Sometimes I felt that he was testing his memory with our conversations. If he slipped, I wouldn't suspect a thing, and he could continue adding color to faded corners, inventing details for whatever eluded him.)

On the last day of the visits, the uncle would pull M. aside and give him what seemed at the time a generous amount of money. He told M. to do as he pleased with this cash, and not bother telling his parents. On one such occasion, after the uncle returned to America, M. went to the pie shop downtown and ordered ten mince pies. He hadn't been able to eat them all, and perhaps he even knew this when he made his order. He guessed, too, that even though his uncle had told him to do as he pleased, he would nevertheless have been surprised by M.'s choice. But this was one of the most wonderful moments of his childhood, M. said. It was not the pleasure of eating, he told me, while we sat with our picnic stretched between us on the bench, but the freedom to do as he wanted. Perhaps, he added, that is also why he wrote.

But most of the time we sat in silence and looked at the water. Sometimes I would look over at M. and he would nod his head up and down, as if he were agreeing with something. I didn't know whether this gesture meant, "You see? You see?" or if he were telling me, "I know, I know."

47.

efore she started going to school, my mother would pack a
schoolbag and go over to Akif amca's. He showed her how
to spell the names of all her family members. My mother sat
at the table, carefully writing out her exercises, and from time to
time Akif amca rattled the contents of a drawer and said that it
was the recess bell.

It is remarkable how ordinary this story is and how devotedly
my mother told it.

"I sat across from him doing the work he gave me, and from
time to time he rang the recess bell."

What is remarkable is that my mother cared enough about
these stories to repeat them.

"At recess, he tied cloth dolls to his fingers and bounced
them about, making me laugh."

When I was a child, I understood clearly and without judgment that my mother told stories about Akif amca because he had loved her abundantly.

But later, I found it pathetic that she still held on to these scraps.

ONE TIME WHEN I WAS IN HIGH SCHOOL, WE WATCHED A MOVIE about another mother and daughter. They slept in the same room and chatted under the covers at night. There was a montage of all the things they did together—walking into photo booths at train stations, cycling in parks, baking pies, having food fights. By the time we became aware of the movie's sentimentality it was too late to turn it off and we watched, embarrassed of each other, until the end.

Afterwards, we continued sitting in the living room without speaking. A new movie came on. Then my mother said, "You know, Nunu, I would go to Akif amca's and pretend that it was a classroom. Did I ever tell you about that?"

I shrugged, pretending to be engrossed in a magazine I'd picked up from the coffee table.

"Actually," she continued, "I always thought of Akif amca as just my playmate, but I think that he was also a very good poet.

"Really," she said. "Next time we're in Aldere we should look at his notebooks. I'm sure you'll be surprised."

I told her I doubted it.

Much later, when I told stories of my mother to Luke, I didn't want to remember anything that might contradict the character I'd created. But I remember now that she was trying, my mother, to find a way to reach me.

48.

For a long time into our knowing each other, several weeks, perhaps some months, M. did not say my name out loud.

And as if to make up for it, he wrote it often in his e-mails, sometimes in succession, playing around with the syllables and composing new meanings: "Nurunisa, Nur-u-nisa, Nur. Nisa." I guessed that he might be uncertain about its pronunciation, even more so because he was embarrassed when I sometimes corrected the way he said a Turkish word, as if I had caught him telling a lie. I don't know why he preferred my full name, even though I had told him that everybody called me Nunu. Even my mother, who rarely granted me childishness, preferred this small word to the old-fashioned name given to me by my father.

I respected M.'s care with words and I resented it. When we came upon a beautiful sight, I would want him to say something that revealed the workings of his imagination. We crossed the river at sunset many times, when the colors gathered and deepened and the sky descended lower onto the city. This sky always made M. pause and I waited for him to speak. But he only stated what I could also see—"Look at the orange tip of that cloud," or "What a mottled sky"—before continuing.

The first time he said my name, we were standing beneath the arcades across from the Senate. At one end was one of the first meter sticks in the city. I had discovered it on my own some days before, when I happened to take shelter from the rain there, and I had brought M. to the same spot to show him.

This was the only meter stick, I had learned, that was still in its original place after the switch to the metric system, when several others were installed around Paris. There was something interesting to me about this, even sad, though I guessed that M. might not immediately see what was so special in a regular meter. I would point out to him the poetry in this simple line drawn on marble: one hundred centimeters on a white wall marking with precision the new order of the city. It was the type of thing Akif amca might have noted in his journal—at least the Akif amca I told M. about, whenever we discussed my Thracian project.

I fiddled with my camera, pretending to focus on the shadows falling diagonally all the way across the arcade. I was waiting for M. to walk towards the meter so that I could tell him about it as I had planned.

I must not have heard that he asked me something. When I didn't reply, he said my name. Perhaps he noticed my expression as I looked up, because he quickly asked whether he was pronouncing it correctly. It was a question one would ask a stranger. He added that he admired the musicality of my name and was afraid to ruin it with his "terrible accent."

I raised the camera to my eyes and pointed it at him. He took a few steps back, so that he was perfectly positioned in front of the white wall, the meter stretching out from either side of his neck.

For some time, I looked at him through the viewfinder, watching his face. He looked down to the ground, then looked up again, waiting for me to take the photo.

I watched for a while longer in the comfortable distance, behind the lens.

"Nurunisa?" he said again.

I took the photograph and put the camera down, just as he leaned back and smiled for the picture.

It's the only one I have of him.

49.

Some evenings, my mother went over to Akif amca's and sat on the floor, in front of the stove by the armchair. While Akif amca read, my mother would draw, or lie on her back and stare at the ceiling. Before he sent my mother back home, Akif amca wound his watch. He told my mother to listen, bringing the watch to his ear, and the two of them held their breaths to hear the sound. Akif amca told my mother that it was rushing to make up for all the lost time. I loved this story and brought my own watch to my ear often during my childhood, listening to the hurrying time.

I asked my mother about this one evening when we were looking through old photographs. This was later, that year I was back in Istanbul. I asked my mother many things in those months, to make up for all the lost time.

I'd realized that I didn't really know what Akif amca's words had meant. I didn't even know whether I remembered the story of the watch correctly or if I had forgotten one of the key moments that tied the pieces together.

In one picture, Akif amca was sitting in his armchair with his legs crossed.

"Remember when Akif amca wound his watch? What would he tell you?"

"What do you mean?" my mother said.

"When he asked you to listen," I said.

My mother said I must be remembering incorrectly. She had never told me this.

But I was certain that she must have forgotten her own story and was even pleased that I now had full ownership of it. I thought that maybe Akif amca had not known the meaning of these words either and was equally enchanted by their elusive poetry.

It was only when I moved to Paris and began looking through the journal for things to tell M. about my Thracian project that I realized Akif amca had been remembering his own lines.

A moment after the invention
the city rushes, to make up for lost time.

50.

Here is something else I learned from M.

In ancient memory exercises, students are advised to place whatever they want to remember inside the chambers of an imaginary building. The building must be spacious and symmetrical and students must shape their memories into striking images and place them one by one inside the evenly spaced rooms.

The solitary walker of this building will doubtless have to distort the memories in order to recall them. Sometimes, the most tedious facts will become marvelous in their unusual forms, displayed in these memory palaces.

Some walkers, M. said, must have been moved by the sights in their own minds, entirely different from their familiar and mundane counterparts in the world. Some must even have wanted to excavate them back out into daylight by committing them to paper, to marble, to walls.

M. sometimes referred to our shared memory palace, where the two of us had invented our own times of day (he always found a different way to bring up "The Invention of Midnight"). The rooms of this building, he said, which contained replicas of the most unremarkable sights, had turned into treasures.

"Don't you think so as well?" he wrote. I was touched by this hopeful question. I can't remember what I wrote back. I don't always have the heart to go back and read my own responses. I didn't think at the time that I was constantly avoiding M.'s words—the very ones that made me happy. I would have said I was waiting for the next note, adding each one to my collection, though it must certainly have appeared as if I were pushing the words away.

This idea of a palace has stayed with me, even if I believe it is too neatly constructed to shed light on the devious ways of memory. Its innocent sleight of hand is only in the amplification of what is remembered, when the truth has so much more to do with hiding and forgetting.

OFTEN AS WE WALKED, THERE WERE THINGS I REMEMBERED fully and in an instant. A childhood joke, the smell of coal in winter, the way a rusty box opens with a slight twist, at a particular spot. I didn't keep a record of all these things, and some I've now forgotten. What's left of the memory is only the knowledge that I'm no longer in possession of something I once knew intimately. It is useless, this residue of absence.

After I moved back to Istanbul—moved back for good—I ran into M. at every corner. I saw him on the ferry, at the juice and burger stands, in coffeehouses along the water. Sometimes, when I look at his photograph, at the raised eyebrows, the scar rising dramatically, I can hardly remember who he was. But every time I caught a glimpse of him in the stares and stoops of strangers, I would know him in an instant.

51.

Before that year I spent with my mother, I had told her that I would never come back to Istanbul. I had my own reasons, something that grew bigger inside me. I have called it silence, even if it made itself known with words.

And there was something else, which felt at the time like confidence, in the life I'd created in London, among people who saw me differently. I thought that I had put things in order and that I could keep them in balance, so long as I kept a distance.

On the phone one evening, my mother told me we should go to the Borsa Restaurant when I came to visit. It had recently been renovated, she said. Did I remember that restaurant inside the Adile Sultan Pavilion? There is such a view of the Judas trees in the spring that it takes your breath away.

"Do you remember, Nunu, you and I went there before?"

Another time she said, "Do you remember our fish lunches?"

What I resented most was not so much the question as the meekness, that false note of sweetness that was not my mother's. At the time, I could not hear her plea.

"As soon as you come back," she said on the phone, "I'm going to take you to the Adile Sultan Pavilion."

"I'm not coming back to Istanbul," I told her.

"Of course, I understand. You should be focusing on your future," my mother said.

"That's not it," I said. I had been practicing what I would say.

"I'm not coming back because I'm learning to forgive and to forget."

IT IS THE STUFF OF FICTION THAT A SINGLE CONVERSATION CAN change the course of a life; that we will return to it again and again, wishing to undo it. Even if we could, so much would remain. There are many ways of hurting, without words. It's silence that shapes us.

My mother must have known about her illness then and she may have felt relief at my words. And I want to say, without an attempt to comfort or pardon myself, that I was so wrapped up in the story I'd been telling Luke, coloring my own memories, that my mother may not even have understood what I was talking about.

52.

After we moved from Moda to the new apartment, on the nights she did not come to stand at my door, I would go to her.

"Nejla," I called from the threshold, but she didn't respond.

I never told Luke about that, all those evenings he and I sat on our quilted bed.

She lived in her own world, I said, far from reality.

I would shake my head as if I had no words for what I felt. Sometimes, I told Luke, my mother would not speak to me for days.

And I was just a child. "Imagine doing that to a child," I would say, bringing tears to my eyes.

Luke might reach over and squeeze my hand.

"You poor Buddyback," he said.

But what I didn't tell him was something far simpler. I would go to my mother's bedroom and call to her from the door. The room would be very dark and my mother would be in terrible pain from one of her headaches. I wouldn't say anything else as I quietly went back to my room.

53.

ooking at the photograph of M. now, I see something new in his expression. Perhaps because it has been several years since that afternoon when we went to see the meter stick beneath the arcades. Today, what I see is neither bewilderment nor annoyance, but expectation. M. is looking at me with anticipation. If only I were to focus, I might be able to see what M. saw when he looked at me.

WE USED TO SIT IN THE COURTYARD OF A MUSEUM BEHIND THE Montparnasse station, converted from the studio of a nineteenth-century sculptor whom M. admired—one of many artists in Paris whose traces were more or less washed away with time, which I think was the very reason for M.'s interest in him. ("Another Apollodorus," we might have called him.) M. had even shown me a book of this sculptor's class notes, which were the transcripts of studio hours when he walked from student to student, pointing out the flaws and strengths in their work, calling their attention to forms they may have missed. These conversations, M. said, with only the words to outline the sculptures in the studio, gave him a pleasure akin to reading a ghost story.

I enjoyed being among the marble crowd of statues, which were mostly reworkings of the same three figures, with pained, serious, or ambivalent expressions. The slight reiterations in their gestures and even clothing created new meaning in each new cast. But the sculptor, M. said, had told the same story his whole life. He said this often, not just about this particular sculptor, but about all artists he admired. In M.'s opinion, these artists told the same story again and again, and unlike Luke, he meant it as a compliment.

One time, as we were leaving, I noticed a sculpture of a naked woman, different from all the others. She had wide hips, and her stone hair was collected on her head in a soft pile. One leg was crossed over the other, a pose that echoed her mischievous smile. In one hand, she was holding an apple, as if it were a ball she was about to throw up in the air.

She was playful with her fruit and her loosely gathered hair, totally unlike the troubled faces around her. It gave me such pleasure to look at her that I stood in front of her for some time, smiling back, jealous, I suppose, of a piece of stone.

After a while, M. came and stood next to me and I realized that I had crossed my legs just like the statue. He didn't say anything, and I kept standing as I had been before, but I felt I was becoming, like the marble, very stiff and that my face and throat were burning.

54.

've made it a habit to leave my apartment a bit early on my way to work each morning. I stop to have tea at a bakery or sit in a park. There are the shopkeepers of Moda who know me by name now. Some call out greetings to me on my way.

For hours at a time each day, I forget that I live in Istanbul. At work, I write about other cities—more beautiful, less troubled. At least one section of every issue of the magazine is dedicated to an unrivaled capital of the world. St. Petersburg, Paris, Florence, Amsterdam. These cities offer readers the surest way to escape their lives for the span of a few pages. They are beautiful, through and through, without anything to hide.

And then there are those waiting to be discovered, waking up after years of hardship, newly bustling: Tbilisi, Warsaw, Riga.

I've become accustomed to summing them up—plazas,

cathedrals, restaurants, myths—packing them tight with charm, inventing superlatives.

"You make me want to go there," Esra often says across the desk from mine. She's the youngest at the magazine. She's never lived anywhere else. "Anyway," she says, "anyplace is bound to be better than here."

I tell her she may be right. I don't want to seem foreign to my colleagues; to marvel like a tourist at the city we should all have had enough of by now.

After completing each issue, we celebrate at the bar across the street, raising our glasses to the same toast: "To travel," one of us says, and the others respond, "To getting the hell out!"

55.

eventually learned that one of the "tasks" keeping M. from devoting all his time to the new book was teaching writing, because I sometimes met him after his class at the university. We'd walk from there down the avenue Bosquet towards Invalides. On those afternoons, when I saw him emerge from the building and descend the stone steps, he appeared like another person, even if he still wore his green jacket and stooped slightly. Sometimes he was with a colleague or with one of his students, and he parted with them cheerfully at the bottom of the steps before crossing the street to greet me with his raised hand. I wonder if I had seen him incorrectly all this time—this stammering man I described.

On those days, M. always had something to tell me about his classes. He took his students' struggles to heart, and worried that he would not be able to teach them to write authentically.

He was troubled, he told me one time, by the difficulty of making his students understand the difference between art and artifice. He said that what the students thought of as style was an unwillingness to tell a story. He wondered whether he was only teaching them the illusory mechanics of craft, by which they could conceal the absence at the heart of their writing, trying to make up for all the things they were not able to confront. I nodded in agreement, but I wondered, feeling uneasy and embarrassed, whether M. was trying to tell me something in his particular way.

56.

On Bayram morning (it must have been the first one since I had come to Paris), I called Saniye and Asuman. They were sad I was spending it alone.

"All alone in those places," they said, the way anyplace outside of Istanbul became plural when it signified separation, as if to underline the impossibility of reaching across the vast distance. I told them they shouldn't worry. I was enjoying myself in Paris, I was learning a lot, I was writing.

I had even met someone, I said. He was a writer, and he wrote books about Istanbul. Until then, during our brief phone conversations, I had not mentioned M.

I told them that M. was a famous writer, knowing they gave importance to such things.

"Is he your teacher from school?" they asked. They didn't know I hadn't been to classes.

"No," I said. "Just a friend. But we go on walks and we talk about writing."

"Where do you walk?" Saniye said.

"All around the city. We have so much to talk about."

"What does this man want from you?" Asuman asked. "What does a grown man want from a young girl, who isn't a writer or anything?"

STORIES HAVE THEIR OWN LOGIC. FOR ONE THING, A STORY CAN only be told once it has an ending. For another, it builds, and then unravels. Each element of a story is essential; its time will come and it will ultimately mean something. In this way, stories are accountable, because they can look you in the eye.

57.

Akif amca had met James Baldwin in Istanbul during an engagement party at the house of two actors. Baldwin arrived uninvited, my mother told me, and even though I didn't know at the time who he was, I still liked this story of an uninvited guest, perhaps for no other reason than my mother telling me a story.

"The black writer James Baldwin," my mother informed me, nevertheless. Then she added, "Who knows how much of this is true." According to Akif amca, people called him "Jimmy the Arab," with the old-world ignorance at a time when Ethiopian nannies to wealthy Istanbul families were called "Arab sisters." I wrote about this to M. It was exactly the type of thing that would delight him.

("The simplest one of your stories," M. once wrote to me, "is more intriguing than all the bohemians in Paris.")

I can't say for certain when I began to boast to M. with the stories I told him. Perhaps it was when we finally dropped the pretense that I was writing a novel about Akif amca, the poet. Little by little, we stopped talking about my project, and M. no longer asked whether I had made any progress in my search for the poet's traces in Paris. But he told me often that I was lucky to have such a wealth of stories at my disposal.

It distressed me to think that M. might have known all along that I'd never intended to write a book about Akif amca, and had only used it as an excuse to become his friend, and tell him stories that weren't quite mine.

Whatever the reason, there was a time when I began to insist that I knew the Istanbul of M.'s books more intimately than he did. This vanished city full of unexpected crossings and a poetic sadness.

I had finally told M. that I'd read one of his novels. I'd come across it at the bookshop where we'd first met, I said, and couldn't resist the temptation.

M. waved his hand in the air, embarrassed, as if he wanted to dismiss the conversation. That modest gesture prompted me to add that I had, in fact, loved the book.

But later, I began to point out small details he'd missed; particularities of the time period he seemed unaware of. I tried to make my comments sound generous, as if I was telling him all this to enrich his world. M. listened to me without objection. He even thanked me.

——

THE STORY CONTINUED THAT BALDWIN HAD FALLEN ASLEEP on the lap of one of the guests. When he woke up, he went to the kitchen and sat at the table to write amidst harried maids assembling platters of fruit.

This was when Akif amca met him, coming through the kitchen to go out to the balcony. Baldwin followed him out, with two glasses of tea. Akif amca recalled the way he held the glass at the rim, with his long fingers. The two men shared a cigarette, watching the city.

Akif amca waited for Baldwin to say something about the view. He wondered what a foreigner thought of Istanbul; whether he found it as beautiful as he did. But Baldwin sipped his tea and looked out at the hills with darting eyes, and from time to time he reached over to take the cigarette from Akif amca.

There was something peculiar about the way my mother told me about the two men on the balcony, which is why I remember it so well.

"Who knows if any of it is true," she said again, the way she sometimes did with resentment, as if she were accusing Akif amca for the stories with which he had filled her happy childhood.

"At the end of his life," my mother said some time later, telling me about Akif amca waiting for Baldwin to praise his city, "this remarkable man's only friend would be a child.

"Poor Akif amca," she said, "standing on that balcony."

———

I'D FELT ENVY FOR AKIF AMCA AND THE LOVE MY MOTHER HAD for him.

SEVERAL DAYS AFTER I WROTE TO M. ABOUT THIS MOMENT ON the balcony, I realized that my description of Baldwin's darting eyes was something I had read in one of M.'s novels, in his passage about the old man watching the city hills. I realized that my phrasing was almost word for word M.'s description of his character. I'd read that scene many times; I even read it to my mother when she was ill—when the old man stands on a balcony looking out at the city spread on the hills.

I didn't write to M. for several days because I felt embarrassed. I was certain that he had noticed my slip, even though he hadn't commented on it. I felt an urge to explain myself, in case he thought that other things I told him were embellished in the same way. But I kept silent, even after M. wrote to propose a day for our walk. After several days of silence, he wrote again, to ask whether I was alright, adding that he missed hearing what treasures I had collected in these past few days to show him.

I wrote back to say that this was in fact the problem. It could be tiring to collect things.

"As if I'm constantly being probed for entertainment," I wrote. "Like a jukebox."

(M. loved jukeboxes. He used them often as metaphors.)

I said this because I was ashamed.

M. wrote back that I should never feel obliged to tell him stories.

"Please don't think you must constantly invent things in order to entertain me," he said. "And please don't feel you have to reveal something to me."

58.

That year in Istanbul, my mother asked me to read to her. This was later, when she no longer got out of bed.

I would sit in the armchair next to her bed and put my feet up on the edge of her mattress. I read until I could hear her heavy breathing. Sometimes when I stopped reading, she reached over and held my toes to let me know that she was still listening. I remember her fingers, so thin they might go right through my feet.

In the afternoon, the bedroom would be very bright and I drew the curtains shut. We would sit like this until the evening, reading or sitting in silence.

"Nunu, why don't you go for a walk?" my mother said when she drifted out of sleep. I pretended I hadn't heard her.

"It would make me happy if you went out a bit."

I wouldn't respond.

"Nunu," she'd say, "you're so stubborn."

I HAD ALREADY FINISHED READING M.'S NOVEL MYSELF WHEN I read her the chapter about the old man on the balcony, looking out with his darting eyes. I can still remember the long description of the city, moving imperceptibly from the old man to the hills in front of him. It's unlike M.'s other indulgences, when he spends pages describing trees and foods. In this passage, the old man's eyes are just an extension of the flickering city.

When he finally jumps off, there seems to be no break in the prose.

It's remarkable to me that a foreigner has seen this loneliness in our city. He has seen right through the hills and waters to the very heart of Istanbul. Such a loneliness it robs you of words.

My mother did not object to these passages as she had objected to M.'s description of the cypresses.

It was late afternoon, and the last bright light filled the room like mist through the already drawn curtains. I rested my feet at the edge of my mother's bed while I read.

The old man's darting eyes settle on the city, which holds out its arms to him in an embrace.

I wanted my mother to hear this, to tell her that the weight did not belong to us alone. That others, strangers even—those so foreign to Istanbul that they wrote about its abundant cypresses—could know something of this feeling we had guarded all our lives. That they, too, could have witnessed such loneliness.

My mother reached over and held my toes with her thin hand.

"Nunu," she said. "Nunito."

59.

I t was on one of the first true days of spring—those days,
which are a festivity in Paris, bringing everyone to café fronts—
that we decided to go for a midnight picnic after M.'s class.
I arrived early, and sat down on the bench across from the
university entrance. I was wearing a green sleeveless dress I
had recently bought, when the weather became warmer and I
began noticing the crowds at cafés shedding their somber lay-
ers. I had put on this dress only once before in my room,
taking pleasure in its deep color, the comfortable sweep and
fall of its skirt, the way it hugged my waist. And I had been so
pleased that I went downstairs to the Café du Coin so someone could see me.

"She's back," the young waiter said when I walked in. He
winked, and brought a cup of coffee without my asking.

M. LEFT THE UNIVERSITY BUILDING WITH THE GOLDEN AGE author, the one who had read at the bookshop. They looked in my direction as they were walking down the steps. M. made no sign that he'd seen me. I got up from the bench. A moment later, he looked up again and this time waved enthusiastically.

When they crossed the street, he held me by the shoulders and kissed me on both cheeks, so unlike the way he usually greeted me. I had become accustomed to the abrupt wave of his hand and I thought that it had its own special meaning.

"Look at you," he said. "What a sight of spring."

He introduced me to the writer as his guide.

"To all things Thracian," he said.

"It's lucky you found a guide," the writer said. "Do you guide tours in other landscapes, too?"

M. laughed.

After we parted with the writer, we walked down the tree-lined avenue Bosquet, dappled with light straining through the leaves. We turned onto rue Cler, where every café terrace was filled with people. All along the pavement, they stood with their drinks, wearing dresses, and pastel-colored trousers.

"What a day," M. said. "Maybe we should sit at a café."

I shrugged.

"I thought we were going for a picnic."

"Of course," he said. "If you prefer."

It wasn't only M.'s introduction that had upset me, but his cheerfulness as well. It made me lonely.

We continued towards the river.

"I'm so glad we're walking," M. said. "And not wasting this splendid day."

It hadn't been splendid until now, he said. That afternoon, one of his students had turned in a story about his family written with such bitterness that it had been uncomfortable to discuss in class.

I asked him why this was.

"At the heart of it, there is shame," M. said. "But it's hidden under so much anger. How do you teach them to tell the story as it is, when they are blind to the very feeling with which they are telling the story?"

I walked silently, looking ahead.

"Sometimes," he said, "I wonder if I'm capable of teaching them the joy of plain, simple storytelling. The way you and I tell each other."

I had stopped walking. I was looking down at the hem of my green dress.

"I don't think you should try and teach anyone how to talk about their family," I said. "It's arrogant."

We continued walking.

"Nurunisa," M. said, "is something the matter?"

I shook my head. But when we reached the American Church, I told him I was not feeling too well.

"What can we do about that?" he asked.

I said I wanted to go home.

I had an urge to be reckless. To cause damage in one sweep.

But I was also trying to stop myself and shake off this feeling before it overcame me.

"Of course," M. said. "I'll walk you to the metro."

As we changed course and continued walking, I decided that if he said something else, anything at all, I would tell him that I wasn't feeling that bad after all, and that I would still like to have our picnic.

I pleaded with him silently until we reached the metro.

"I hope you feel better," M. said, and waved.

60.

So much falls through the cracks when I try to tell it. So much insignificant detail. There are many little things that don't have a place in a story.

My mother used to wear glasses with blue and green dots. She had these glasses for as long as I can remember and they never lost their bright color. When she put them on, I can't say why, it made me happy. Those bright colors framing my mother's eyes and my mother's determination—to read something, to write something, to find a way to be cheerful. She could set everything aside and give her attention to a single task when she wore her glasses.

"Let's see now," she would say, putting on her glasses when I brought her my homework, or my school skirt with a loose button.

In moments like this I wondered whether my mother wasn't

just going about her life, whether I had only imagined that there was something darker hovering over her. I wonder whether I could have told a different story of my mother all along, about the ordinary course of a life, with its ordinary list of sadness and joy.

61.

I'm trying to say that I've tried to tell a story about her many times. But none have resembled my mother.

62.

We met again at the Luxembourg metro, we walked around the gardens. We sat down for lunch, we went to our bench. I doubt that change comes sweeping in a single moment. I think it is always there, waiting for the right time to make itself known.

Still, if I had to trace our path back to some specific time, mark it as different from others who came before and after, I would remember the festive day when I wore that green sleeveless dress, when M. seemed like a stranger and we stepped out of our world. It must be around this time that I stopped writing to him, except practically, to set a time to meet. But even this, I cannot say for certain. M. still wrote to me in his particular way, repeating my name.

"Nurunisa, Nur-u-nisa, Nur. Nisa."

One time he wrote, "Silent one with her head down."

And another time, "Nurunisa across the river: Have you dropped our invisible thread?"

I had made up my mind that once he asked me directly why I was upset, I would tell him a true story, something simple and direct. This was the condition I had set and I waited impatiently for him to understand, to want to know and admit he cared. I don't even know what I would have told him if he asked. But the question itself would have assured me that M. was the person I thought I knew.

After a while, though, M. stopped writing to me.

63.

At first, the silence was heavy, as if I could hear M. acknowledging it across the city. Later, it grew lighter. M. slipped into another silence, entirely his own. With time, it became commonplace and we were no different than two strangers on a street.

I was relieved, and then saddened. Later, I was angry that M. would give up so easily. I told myself that our friendship had ended once M. had collected enough material for his book and no longer needed me.

That's one way of telling it. I know there are others.

64.

I remember this story my grandmother told, without embellishments from me, as improbable as it seems: My grandfather had drawn the plan of the house in Aldere on the square pack of his Bafra cigarettes, and divided the square into quarters. He had given the plan, just as it was on the cigarette pack, to the workers at the factory to build. Whenever she compared herself to Europeans, my grandmother would say, sighing deeply, that her life was worth no more than a pack of cigarettes.

65.

I n the end, Istanbul welcomed me back with open arms.

I returned from Paris to Atatürk Airport and stepped outside to the familiar smell of cigarette smoke.

I took a taxi and gave the driver the aunts' address in Kanlıca. I had forgotten about the traffic. For an hour, we moved inch by inch on the highway.

The radio was announcing the trial of three journalists whose names were not familiar to me. I could neither think of conspiracies nor deeper connections that might help me read a larger meaning into this event. The driver made a clucking sound and shook his head from side to side, switching to another channel, and I didn't know whom he disapproved of with this gesture.

All along the road were turns leading to housing projects with foreign names—City Verde, City Soleil, Flora Plaza. In banners suspended from buildings, there were photographs of spacious, tree-lined streets and modern buildings without a trace of life. I felt as if I had walked into a trap. I had returned to a place that had nothing to do with me.

But after a while, the highway narrowed. There was a quickening, a coming to life, a descent into something I could not put my finger on. My surroundings looked familiar, even though I could still not say what road we were merging onto. Finally, the strait appeared ahead, and I saw the bridge. I had not expected to see it at that moment, that sparkling water, the hills below, and the fortress slithering magnificently up and along the curving banks. That blue-green of the Bosphorus, whose color I have never seen elsewhere. The city spread its wings, falling steeply and stretching wide, welcoming me with its giant arms.

And in its embrace it told me something, like the complaint of a child who allows herself a single moment of indulgence. I heard it clearly.

When my mother told me a story from her past, I would wonder why that version of herself didn't match the person I knew in life. I accepted that so much had happened before me. And I was always aware of that threshold between the two times.

In my mother's stories, there was always this same silent accusation that I heard when I arrived in Istanbul.

Look what happened to me.

66.

Soon after I returned to Istanbul from Paris, I received an e-mail from my university roommate, Molly. After graduation, Molly had lived for a while with her parents before moving to Edinburgh.

"It's not the Galápagos," she wrote. "But that's alright."

She told me that she wouldn't mind leading a mediocre life, leave nothing behind and disturb nothing; simply live and be content.

I had been in touch with Molly around the time of my mother's illness and immediately following her death. Afterwards, Molly wrote periodically to ask how I was doing, but I was unable to recall the person I had been around her and I felt it would be strange to write back with facts about my life, without a hint of how she'd known me at university.

"My sad and brave Nunu," Molly wrote to me. "I don't know

what to say. I remember how close you were. I have never known a relationship like yours."

She went on to list the things she remembered about me and my mother. "All your magical landscapes," she said, remembering our Sunday walks, our fish restaurant, the small town by the forest where, she said in a version unknown to me, my mother and I went fishing with my mother's old friend.

She added that she had always regarded my bond with my mother with admiration. Even though she had never met her, she felt that she had gotten to know her through my stories. She said that my remarkable mother had taught her something about living fully. She often thought about our relationship, and had even strived to achieve something similar with her own parents. She'd wanted to offer them friendship as I did to my mother.

I shut the computer, quickly, as if I had seen something indecent.

I DID NOT WRITE TO MOLLY AGAIN FOR A LONG TIME, EVEN though she continued to send me news of her life. Then, I got the note from her when I returned to Istanbul, though she seemed completely unaware that I had only recently come back. She said she was writing to see how I was doing, that she was worried about me. I had been on her mind more and more and she hoped that I was alright, with everything that was happening.

Her concern confused me at first. Enough time had passed since my mother's funeral and Molly knew nothing of my life since then. I didn't know what she assumed, whether she interpreted my long silence in some particular way. I wrote back to tell her I was doing well. I had moved to Paris after the funeral and had just returned to Istanbul.

Molly's response took me by surprise. She was following the events in Istanbul and she imagined what I must be going through, with the city I loved so much coming apart before my eyes. Was I worried? What was my life like?

I was relieved. Of course, Molly would be thinking about Istanbul, and would be worried about my life here, at the brink of uncertainty. These days, there is little room for any other discussion. And it's comforting to give myself up to this change. There is a comfort in insignificance, in the certainty that my own worries will all vanish without a trace.

The troubles of this city surpass us all.

67.

One day, shortly before I left Paris, I asked the waiter at Café du Coin whether he always made a point of bringing me a different type of coffee than what I had ordered.

"Of course," he said. "To check if you're paying attention."

When I was leaving, I saw him smoking outside and asked for a cigarette. The following day, after he ended his shift, he came and sat with me while I finished my coffee.

A few days later we went to see a movie close to Place de la République. The streets were full of people my age, smoking all along the pavements, sitting at run-down bars. It was beautiful in a different way from the neighborhoods M. and I walked repeatedly. Our walks, the stories I told M., our shared vocabulary suddenly seemed far away and irrelevant.

The movie was about a painter and his model who were

separated during the First World War. They found each other again, through a series of improbable events, many years later. By then they were both very old, though they acknowledged that time could do nothing to sever their bond. They remembered every detail of the past. The painter recalled the red dress his model wore on their walks along the river and in the final scene, the old woman who was once a great beauty sat in a park wearing a red dress.

The waiter, Vincent, told me afterwards that he found the story very touching. After all those years, the woman was no longer beautiful, he said, and the painter didn't even mind. This was simply remarkable, Vincent said.

I didn't contradict him, nor did I say that I didn't think the weight of the film resided in the woman's vanished beauty, as I might have told M. It felt good to simply hear his opinion and let it go.

We went to a bar in Oberkampf and sat outside on stools. Once again, I had the feeling that another city had passed me by all this time.

Vincent asked me what I wanted to drink and I told him he could pick. He came back with a tall glass, striped with many colors and with a straw inside, and for some reason the sight of this made me laugh.

"What's so funny?" Vincent said and I couldn't stop laughing at the striped glass—the cheerful drink like children's stationery.

When I finished my drink, he took the colored straw and

tied it around his wrist like a bracelet. I stared at his hands, the jutting veins and muscles. Such a sight, like he was about to break through his own skin.

Afterwards he walked me home, joking the whole time that he'd forgotten to hang up his apron at Café du Coin.

"Usually I can't be bothered to walk beautiful women home," he said. "But this time it's an emergency, with my apron and everything."

We were walking in the middle of an empty street when he reached for my hand and pulled me towards himself. I'd forgotten that things could happen like this—playfully, without solemnity.

When we went up to my room, he stood looking around him, his hands in his pockets.

"So, this is where you escape every time," he said. "Did you bring the old man up here as well?"

He must have noticed the look on my face because he quickly added, "It's really nice of you to be his friend."

This, too, made me laugh.

SOMETIMES, I FIND A WORD THAT SUMS UP A SITUATION. IT comes to me suddenly, often in the voice of the aunts. "She's old-fashioned," I heard them saying, as if there was nothing else to be made of the situation. I thought with relief that my friendship with M. was simply old-fashioned. It was this incongruity, I decided, that had drifted us apart.

A few days later at the café, Vincent asked my landlord, "Where did you find such a giggly tenant?

"At first we thought you were a bit strange," he continued. "But now we find out you were laughing at us all along."

When I was leaving Paris, Vincent said he would think of me in Istanbul.

"And you think of me at Café du Coin, making your coffee the wrong way," he said.

68.

The last time I saw M. was at a discussion, at the same book-shop where I'd first met him a year before. Once again, there were signs announcing the event at the shop front, and I was a bit surprised that M. had not told me about it, even if we hadn't spoken for some time.

I don't know whether he saw me when I entered the room a few minutes after the discussion started. The bookshop was completely full, and I stood at the back, with a partial view of the row of speakers.

The writers were asked to talk about their routines, the ways they found inspiration, that sort of thing. The famous writer was there again, seated next to M. He had not published anything else since his book about Paris's golden age.

He spoke at length about his rituals of writing. "I think of it as a rite of passage," he said. "I enter a different world with different rules. But in order to enter that world, I must first be admitted."

He had a particular notebook, a pencil, a time of the day. There were the poems that he read again and again.

"Basically," he said, "I do everything I can to prepare myself before stepping into the unknown."

When it was M.'s turn, he said that he admired his colleague's conviction that the story was out there, just beyond his reach, if only he was determined enough to enter its world.

"For me," M. said, "stories are fickle. I must often resign myself to the knowledge that they have their own logic. I am almost powerless in shaping a story because, like people, they do not submit to my expectations.

"The difficulty," he continued, and I thought that he cast a glance towards the back of the room, "is to observe them from afar, in their own worlds. If I can manage to do this, without interfering in my clumsy ways, I am rewarded with sights of an extraordinary beauty. I think that these sights are certainly not the work of my hazy imagination, but things that the mind has noticed and stored away. With care and patience, they reemerge in writing. And sometimes, if I'm delicate enough, I may reach over to hold one and commit such a story to paper.

"But there are many which escape my grasp," he said. "Perhaps it's because I haven't been gentle enough, and they shy back to their own worlds, like photographs of fairy sightings that used to be so popular at one time."

"And other times," he continued, "I'm simply too deaf to hear them."

I noticed, once again, how tall M. was. He was standing straight, without a hint of the stoop with which I have described him. And his voice, too, had nothing of a stammer. I could see that this was M. the writer. This gentle, generous stranger.

69.

remember the sunlight filtering softly on the tables at our bistro. Au Petit Suisse, I mean, across from the Luxembourg Gardens. The light grew gradually, sweeping the tables inch by inch in dusty stripes. I think of this time as in a dream.

In Istanbul, rain comes pouring down, the sun appears without warning. It's hard to remember the moment that came before. The city itself changes so rapidly—buildings sprout up like mushrooms, a new face emerges each day on television screens and newspapers. There is no telling which neighborhood will be demolished to be built anew, what small and unbeautiful park set up beside a looming tower while the ancient trees disappear.

There are the proposed changes, the proposed bills, constructions, state appointments. There are the tunnels, bridges, and metro systems connecting the city from one part to the other, to places I had never known about or been to. There are new rules every day, identity cards, social security systems, shortcuts to pay for entry and exit. A new routine invented daily. There are the faces of politicians about whom I know nothing, who are familiar only in their abundance. Their voices rise some pitches higher above the hum, trying to drown it out.

But I feel something for all these lonely people I see—so lonely amidst such crowds. I feel their dislike of the past, their wish to bury it and to look away. They seem so desperate in this clambering, rising city. In one stroke, they will get rid of anything that has aged. It's a desire for all to be new. It isn't unlike fear.

None of that has a place in the story I'm telling, this world that is changing, this country at the threshold. But it's hard to remember the Istanbul of previous times. The Istanbul of Akif amca, of my mother, of M.'s novels.

I HAVEN'T READ M.'S NEW THRACIAN NOVEL, AND I HAVEN'T made an effort to follow its reception by Turkish readers. The thought of reading it makes me sad. It would be like making a trip to Istanbul's historic peninsula, to visit the palaces and cisterns, to look up at tiles and mosaics and see very little else. To see only that city which is oblivious to change.

But more than this, it seems pointless. There is the hum that deafens all other noise. I imagine that M. will have looked past this, back to another, lovelier time. What use is it to read that, now, when we are at the brink of something, waiting?

I understand the futility of my story at such a time. But then

I imagine our bistro, that striped light, and I worry about everything that will disappear unless I record it.

SOME WEEKS AGO, ON MY WAY BACK FROM THE MAGAZINE, I went into a bookshop before going home. I was the sole customer in the early evening. The bearded, spectacled owner and his cat were absorbed in their business, and I sat for a long time, going through a pile of books by my side. When I was paying for the ones I'd settled on, the owner asked whether I had read the Istanbul books of the English or Irish writer—"I can't recall his name," he said, "it's on the tip of my tongue."

He told me that my selection of books brought to mind this author, whose name he was trying to remember. He had just written a new book, the shopkeeper said, once again set in Turkey. He couldn't remember the title of that one, either.

"Does this happen to you as well," he asked, "when you forget the most obvious things?"

"I don't think I know this author," I told him, but of course I was tempted. I wanted to boast, to tell the shopkeeper that this author had once told me he would never get tired of my stories.

But I will say this. The book's short title is M.'s special way of greeting me, raising his hand for just a moment before putting it back into the pocket of his green jacket. He wants me to understand, even if I don't have the heart to read it, that this is his way of telling the story, his own invention of *Midnight*.

70.

In Paris, after I no longer saw M., I would go to the Gare du Nord and stand by groups of men smoking by the arched glass doors. I already knew then that I would be leaving soon. I had received a note from the program to inform me that my registration was annulled.

I watched the newcomers to the city—businessmen hailing taxis, older and impeccably groomed couples rolling expensive suitcases, lovers reuniting amidst crowds without a care. I didn't have the chance to observe them for long enough to know whether they had arrived in the city in elated spirits or in mourning, just as the visitors themselves did not know whether great joy or misfortune awaited them.

I had always liked the feeling that I could board a train and leave the city whenever I wanted. I liked the idea of arriving at a new place, and the brief period of time when my foreignness would be legitimate.

Sometimes I walked to the slender Gare de l'Est, where trains to Istanbul once departed. Or I walked south, all the way down Sébastopol to the river, past the Luxembourg Gardens (the Judas trees, once again, were barren), the observatory, and then farther out, to the peripheries where the stately apartments of the past century gave way to concrete buildings, the tree-lined streets merged with bridges and highways. I walked to the ancient slaughterhouses at the city's southern gate, whose grounds were converted to the modest Parc Georges-Brassens. It was the type of park one would find in less beautiful cities. There was an artificial pond and gazebo, a brightly colored play area, benches arranged around bronze statues. In those cities, such a park would be the crowning jewel. But in Paris, the Brassens park was almost always deserted.

Some days I traced the periphery of the inner city to the north, past the train station to Belleville, with its garish banquet halls, the alleys and passageways of a vanished working class, concrete buildings inhabited now by migrants. I walked up crowded boulevards, discount stores, electronics shops, hair salons, travel agencies. Beneath overpasses, groups of men sat in tents and on mattresses, surrounded by a clutter of makeshift tables and cardboard roofs. I felt as if I were looking through the invisible walls of a building, seeing into people's homes— plastic bags, paper cups, toothbrushes, blankets, and pillows.

I think that Paris was also changing at that time. Fear and distrust seeped in from every corner. But I did not mind the change so much, or I ignored it. This wasn't really my city, after all, and change does not pain strangers in the same way.

FOR A LONG TIME AFTER THE END OF OUR FRIENDSHIP, I WOULD still talk to M. as I walked. I did it unintentionally, and I would realize with surprise that I had crossed half the city telling him my observations. I still catch myself looking at something and putting it away—collecting it—with the feeling that I'm saving it to show someone later.

After M. and I stopped writing, I wouldn't walk our usual path along the river. The parade of domes, statues, and bridges made me restless; I wanted to be in other streets, where life continued without ceremony.

One morning, I came across the abandoned train tracks that circumscribed the city. I followed three teenagers climbing a low wall, down to the tracks overrun with weeds and broken glass bottles. We walked together for a while, and then the teenagers put down their bags and took out spray paints. I continued past them, until I reached a tunnel. I decided to take a few steps inside, where it was still light. I heard the echoes of my footsteps on the gravel and I continued, soon swallowed by the darkness and the sound. I walked until the tunnel's bright mouth diminished to a frowning pout and sat for a while in complete silence.

The city continued its course above me, inhaling and exhaling, uniting and dispersing, and I felt that I, too, was a small part of it. It was a feeling I had in my childhood, when I found a way to walk on the ceiling.

IT MUST HAVE BEEN IN THE LAST YEAR OF MY FATHER'S LIFE that I began my walks on the ceiling and discovered the white city. I didn't tell anyone of its existence and visited it sparingly on the days when my father did not get up from the armchair and my mother would tell him to stop his games. It was a place I went to when Istanbul was heavy and dark, pressing in against the walls of our apartment.

On those days, I would find the square mirror in my parents' bedroom and take it out of its cloth bag. I put on my mother's wide summer hat, which swallowed my head and restricted my vision. I held the mirror to the ceiling and looked inside, making sure that no part of myself appeared in the reflection.

When I finally saw the white city on the ceiling, I stood still for a while, getting my bearings. I circled the mirror around, observing the stone desert I had landed in. When I was oriented, I tilted the guiding compass of my mirror and started my walk on the ceiling.

First, I traced the undemanding edges of the room. After a while, when I grew accustomed to the landscape, I ventured towards the chandelier growing like a tree in the hallway. To get there, I had to climb the tall ledge between the bedroom and the hallway, raising my legs high so I wouldn't trip. Even though my feet didn't feel the obstacle in front of them, I knew that the invisible rules of the city had to be respected. I had never tried

touching the trunk of the chandelier, either, because my searching feet would merely be met with air. And I knew, when my legs
hit upon objects I couldn't see in the mirror, that the city was
revealing its mysterious sights.

The white city required patience. It had to be walked slowly.
Otherwise, the traveler would stumble and fall, or would see
nothing but her own reflection. If the expedition was carried out
in haste, if a weightless ledge was not carefully stepped over or a
sightless and heavy mountain not avoided (in the real world this
would be an ordinary table or chair), the city would disintegrate.
The white city had to be walked blind but with open eyes.

If I heard anyone approaching, I quickly turned the mirror
down and brought myself back. Sometimes I felt guilty that I
hid this place from my parents. But I was the only one who understood its laws and I did not want to bruise it with clumsy
footsteps.

Besides, I knew that my parents had their own invisible places
where they did not take me. Their cities were also entered on
faith. You had to be certain of their existence, that they were
waiting for you even when you couldn't see them day to day.

Just as my father had been on that night he walked all the
letters of my name, past my mother in the bedroom to the balcony, and then stepped off, leaving us behind.

71.

Despite everything I've said about Istanbul, its new and maddening hum, there is also everything that remains. We don't talk about this, out of fear. To keep envious eyes at bay. But then a ruin sticks out its head from some street. A modest church that has witnessed every civilization; a humble bathhouse; the rose-colored veins of a marble fountain. A street seller looks on idly. A waiter ushers you in, past the heads of smiling fish.

Then the city opens its arms, its blue-green waters.

72.

A kif amca writes of a walk in Paris that he took shortly before he returned to Turkey. This is the last record, if such things can be determined with precision, of a time before he knew my mother.

On this afternoon years ago, Akif amca walks along the river and stops to look at the cathedral from Pont de la Tournelle, before crossing to the Left Bank.

It's a gray afternoon in April. Akif amca writes that even after he leaves the city, nothing will change of the sellers chatting at the Saint-Médard market, the cafés filling up and emptying along the boulevard, the narrow street that is always in shadow, descending to the river. This must be the same street M. and I walked that first night.

People will come together and they will separate, but the

city, Akif amca writes, will remain. I don't know whether the thought fills him with hope or sadness.

I HAD TOLD M. ABOUT THIS LAST WALK IN PARIS RECORDED IN Akif amca's journal. One time, when we stopped on the bridge to look across the water at the cathedral, M. asked if this might be the very spot where our poet stood.

"Which poet?" I asked.

"The great inventor," he said.

That's how I remember our friendship. We passed our stories back and forth until they merged. And with each pass, we lightened our own burden. At that time, brief though it was, we shared a single imagination.

We may even have exaggerated our enthusiasm for the stories we told, for the sake of going on another walk and extending our frail acquaintance a bit further. But in the best moments our friendship was weightless—a pure, untainted invention.

What mattered most was that memory was stripped of bitterness and retold with joy. And once it took root, it grew bigger, this story of how things had been. It was a voice speaking through us, inexhaustible, it seemed, past resentment and sorrow. Past all that could not be resurrected.

ACKNOWLEDGMENTS

Thank you to my agent, Sarah Bowlin, for reading this book by the ocean. To my editor, Laura Perciasepe, for hearing Nunu's voice when it was faint, and for all your suggestions.

Thank you, Lavina Lee, for your thorough reading. To Claire McGinnis, Calvert Morgan, and everyone at Riverhead for their enthusiasm and for bringing this book to life.

For your ideas, intuitions, encouragement, and reading, thank you, Fuat, Vera, Marie, Zsófi, Liz, Gigi, Yuri, Éva, Eda, Nicholas, Katia. I'm so lucky to have you as my friends and readers.

Thank you, Zach, for every afternoon coffee; for the photographs.

For your support and generosity over the years, my Tepoztlán family: Magda, Janet, Anneke, Adriaan, Doug, Rebecca, Kavita.

Thank you, Jonathan, for the first encouragement and for all the walks.

To *Guernica* magazine, for publishing an early chapter of this book.

To the books and their writers who showed me the way: Elizabeth Strout, Enrique Vila-Matas, Patrick Modiano, Georgi Gospodinov, Marilynne Robinson.

İsmihan, Püren hala, Dede, Anneanne, Babaanne, Attila abi, Sergei Sergeevich and Dieuwke, thank you for your stories.

To my parents, Neşe and Serdar, thank you for your love and belief. Thank you, also, for sharing your memories.

To my first reader, Maks. For everything.